For Lisa ~
With special thanks! ♡
Much love ~
Elizabeth Ancona

Spies, Lies & Teacups

Elizabeth Ancona

United Writers Press
Asheville, N.C.

ISBN: 978-1-945338-61-8

First Edition: August 2019

Published by
United Writers Press
Asheville, N.C.
www.UnitedWritersPress.com

Printed in the United States of America.

Castle icon made by Freepik from www.flaticon.com
Other icons licensed from shutterstock.com

To Christopher,
who loves me more than himself

Contents

1

To New Beginnings

England was just as I always imagined it—except it was actually way better. Sam and I were practically fainting from jetlag, but I was too excited. It had been a great first day in England so far, and although my brain was fuzzy and the 18th century converted carriage house we were staying in was charming, I didn't want to waste a minute in our hotel sleeping—I wanted to get out and see the English sites I'd always read about and seen in movies.

I was overwhelmed with the number of adorable pubs close by. Where would I have my first meal in England? The fancy Duchess of Cambridge with its arched doorways, hanging baskets and pale blue-green walls? Or the red brick Carpenter's Arms, covered in window boxes with a sign that said it was founded in 1518? Better yet, the Two Brewers with my favourite exterior of climbing pink roses, prolific window boxes, and a bower of hanging baskets?

Sam sighed. "Marion, just pick one. I'm starving."

The Two Brewers was next to Windsor Castle and the Long Walk. I thought we could take a stroll and follow the path of King Henry VIII after lunch.

I stopped in front. "Okay, let's eat here, but take a picture of me in front of the pub first." I handed him my smartphone and got into position. "Do you see the sign and the flowers, and do you see the tables out front, and can you see the castle behind me?"

Sam sighed again. "Yes, I have everything in the picture, and I got you, too."

I returned the phone to my purse and squeezed Sam's arm. "Thank you again and again for bringing me here!"

We opened the door and stepped back in time into the dark pub. When my eyes adjusted, I saw low ceilings, quirky little rooms that seemed hodge-podged together, and wooden tables set against walls covered with photographs that spoke of days gone by.

Sam led me over to a table for two in the corner by a fireplace filled with lighted candles. I guessed summer was too early to have a fire although it seemed cool enough compared to the Ohio temperatures we'd left behind. He pulled out a wooden chair and sat down. I hesitated, glancing toward the bar. "Shouldn't you ask the hostess if we can sit here?"

Sam grinned and gestured to the other chair. "This isn't America. After a couple a blundering business trips here, I finally figured out how to get served at a pub. You seat yourself and then you go up to the bar to order and pay. Then a waitress brings the food. We carry our own drinks back to the table."

"That's really strange."

"No, that's British. They've been doing this restaurant gig a lot longer than we have." He leaned over and kissed my forehead to take the edge off my embarrassment at the cultural lesson.

I glanced up at a blackboard with the menu for the day. "Can we get fish and chips and a pint?"

"That sounds good to me," he said.

He left me at the table and went to the bar to order. I amused myself looking at black and white photographs of various scenes around Windsor Castle and the Thames River. One other couple sat at a table nearby, and I eavesdropped for a moment. I loved hearing their proper English accents.

Sam returned to the table bearing two glasses of beer—one smaller than the other. He set the smaller in front of me.

"Your beer looks enormous," I said.

He nodded. "Mine's a pint. I got you a half." He grabbed his glass and lifted it into the air. "Cheers! To a fun and relaxing six weeks of holiday with the most beautiful woman in the world!"

I tried to sit back and enjoy the ambience and the murmur of British voices around me, but for the past twelve months any time something good happened, I became overwhelmed with tears and guilt that Wills—William, our firstborn son and my parents' first grandson—wasn't there to enjoy it with us. Even the surroundings of a new country and culture couldn't keep the dark thoughts away. I slipped back in time, hearing the noisy banter in the car on the way to the soccer game.

William hoped that the rain would stop so the game wouldn't be canceled. I'd only taken my eyes off the road for one second to glance in the rear-view mirror at the car behind me. Its headlights had come up too close and I'd slowed down to let it pass, but another car had approached from the other direction, and I had been forced off the road. William had taken off his seatbelt to put on his cleats and had taken all the impact. He'd died at the scene.

I didn't see the tree we crashed into that day, but it had appeared every night in my dreams for months afterward and still flashed in front of my eyes in random moments.

I shuddered even though the pub was warm. Sam noticed and put his arm around me. "Cheers to today," he said again, responding to what I suppose was the look on my face. Still holding the glass, he continued. "I loved how you talked to that teenager who was sitting on the plane next to us. You knew exactly how to help him with the movie player without making him feel dumb. And, of course, you had snacks in your purse for him. You're not only the most beautiful woman, you're the best mom to our sons and everyone else's son." He lifted his glass again. "To our sons, William and Bear."

I paused, shaking away the image in my mind, and once again hearing the lovely accents surrounding us. "To William and Bear," I said and touched his glass with mine.

I was glad Sam respected my emotions and patiently waited when I engaged a young man in conversation just because he had a physical feature or was about the same age as Wills. The only positive aspect of the past year was that Sam and I had learned in our grief recovery counseling how to communicate better with each other and share our emotions. The rate of divorce is high after the loss of a child, and we were united in not wanting to make anything worse for our other son.

Bear's real name is Andrew, but he was such a chunky baby and toddler that we nicknamed him Baby Bear. His later love of Paddington Bear stories would cement the nickname, but we dropped the "Baby" part when he'd eaten his way into the body of a muscular athlete over six feet tall.

I was also glad Sam suggested we spend our first few days in one of the smaller towns outside of London so I could experience the culture without all the tourists. Even though I was one of those dreaded tourists and couldn't wait to see all the top tourist sites, it was fun for me to try and blend in as much as I could, often trying to speak with an English accent.

Imitating accents is my one "party trick." Freya, my roommate at university, was from England. She'd come to Ohio for a year as part of a study-abroad program. We had spent hours together perfecting each other's accents and slang. I loved the way she spelled things too, and used the British versions. After that, I'd taken up mimicking accents as a hobby. Friends and strangers usually giggled at me, but both of my boys just moaned that I was embarrassing them. Once in a while, a native of Canada, France, or Australia would compliment my accent attempts, vindicating me.

After graduation, Freya and I had kept in touch despite all the years of living across the pond from each other, working and raising our families. The last time I'd seen her was when she'd come back to America to be the maid of honor in Sam's and my wedding. She'd invited me to fly to Bath to be in her wedding several years later, but I had been hugely pregnant with William and my doctor hadn't wanted me to fly overseas when I was so close to my due date.

We'd written each other letters, which turned into postcards when life got really busy, and then dwindled to Christmas cards. She'd waited later than I did to have children, so her two were still in elementary school. We'd connected on Facebook and that made it easier to keep up our long-distance friendship.

I'd sent her a message that Sam and I were finally coming to England, and she'd invited us to her home in Bath. We would go there in a few days.

A thin young woman with a blond ponytail set down plates of glistening golden-fried fish and thick cut chips—or fries—as we would say back home. A little mound of green peas rested beside the pale food, giving the plate a shot of colour. "Do you need anything else? Tomato sauce, brown sauce?"

I remembered Freya always missed having HP Brown Sauce, and

I never knew what it was. I responded in my best English accent. "Yes, please…some brown sauce and malt vinegar."

"Vinegar's on the table," said the waitress in a distinctly non-British accent. She stalked away before I could ask her where she was from, so I asked her when she returned.

She answered with one word. "Poland."

I was dying to ask her questions about Poland and listen more closely to her accent, but she hurried back to the bar. I turned to Sam. "She sounds just like the woman who checked us into our hotel."

He nodded and explained that since the European Union had opened up, Eastern Europeans had found work in England, especially in the service industries. "All that might change because of Brexit," he said, "but most of the wait staff and hotel workers aren't British."

I was disappointed. "I hope we get to hear lots of *real* English people."

Sam smiled and doused his fish with malt vinegar. "Don't worry. There are plenty of proper Brits about."

We both ate quickly. It had been a long time since the pitiful breakfast we'd had on the plane that morning—and I was in heaven. The fish crunched at first and then melted in my mouth, and the chips were the perfect savory contrast. When the waitress came back to pick up our empty plates, I tried to get her to speak some more.

"How long have you lived here? Did your family move here, too?"

She wouldn't bite. "Six months," she said. "And, no."

I gave up and focused on Sam. "I'm glad we're here for so long. Two weeks in England, two weeks in France, and two weeks in Italy. It seems so long and luxurious. I still can't believe it!"

Two weeks before, Sam had come home early from a business trip. He'd looked tired and worried, but I felt like that had become our new normal physical and emotional state. After he'd put his suitcase and briefcase upstairs in the bedroom, he had come back down and tried to hug me. I'd stiffened and awkwardly hugged him back—that was our new normal, too.

"You're home early," I said.

"Yes, the project wrapped up easier than expected, and I wanted to get back home as soon as I could." He pointed to the small wine rack on the counter. "Let's have a glass of wine."

I'd dutifully sliced some cheese and put out the crackers and salami I kept on hand for easy snacking while he opened a bottle of pinot noir. He'd been unusually tender with me, stroking my hands and face. He'd played with my hair—which he hadn't done in ages—and leaned over to kiss my forehead. I had almost relaxed, but skepticism overtook me. Had he been fired? Was he gearing himself up to tell me more bad news?

My bad news tolerance was pretty much saturated at that point, but he seemed so vulnerable. I heard my mother's voice in my head admonishing me to worry only about today. "Don't dwell on yesterday. Avoid thinking about tomorrow. Today is enough. You can manage today."

She was right. My usually unromantic husband wanted to hug and kiss me and share a glass of wine with me, so I melted. Then, after asking me about Bear, my mom, and what was going on in town, he handed me an envelope. "I've wanted to do this for a long time. I kept meaning to, but the timing never seemed right with your job, my job, the boys, soccer…" He paused. "Happy anniversary?"

I made a face. "Anniversary? That's not for two more months."

Sam looked at me over his reading glasses and smiled. "It's meant as a late anniversary present from all the years I've missed." Quickly, I squashed down the memories of birthdays and anniversaries—once even a Christmas—when Sam had not been there.

I'd opened the envelope to find airline tickets to London, Paris, and Rome. Six weeks together! It was the perfect surprise.

I'm the typical armchair traveler who watches travel videos and reads travel books, imagining a life far away from laundry, housework, after-school practice, before-school practice, meetings and training seminars.

Sam, though, whose job took him all over the globe, had always said he hated traveling. When he came home from a work location I considered exotic, he never wanted to talk—just wanted to sleep, watch the boys play, and eat at home. "I've never seen anything interesting," he always said, "just the insides of planes, hotels, and office buildings and those look the same everywhere."

I wasn't sure if I believed him, but to William and Bear it was like Christmas Day whenever their dad came home, and I wasn't going to spoil it. After all, how could I complain? We had a reasonable income that was probably higher than most. I did part-time hours as a nurse at a pediatric clinic. I was home in the afternoons and weekends for the boys and all their activities.

My mother lived two streets away and she was actually the one who always cast doubts about Sam. "Do you think he has a second family, Marion? He's gone so much, and you can't reach him when he's gone." She had planted that seed in different variations over the years and I had always rebuffed her.

"Mom, don't be dramatic. You watch too much TV. He's always on different time zones." I had to admit, though, that despite my protests, the idea had stubbornly hung around.

I slipped my arm around Sam's and laid my head against his shoulder. "What should we do after lunch?"

"I thought we could head back to our hotel for a nap and then do a late afternoon tour of Windsor Castle. They stay open longer in the summer."

I snuggled into my sweater and laughed at the thought that to

Brits, this cool temperature was considered summer, but before I could say anything about it, Sam held his finger up to the waitress. She came towards us bearing two sparkling glasses of champagne.

He squeezed my hand and lifted his glass. "Before we head back to the hotel, I want to have a toast. To a new start for us, a new beginning to our marriage, an empty nest with Bear off to his freshman year of college and…to forgetting the past."

My stomach lurched painfully at his last words. For months any and everything made me think of Wills, and I would break down in heaving sobs. I wanted to go back in time to when Wills was with us or go forward to this mysterious time that would eventually heal all wounds, but the present was still sometimes unbearably painful.

After a year, my mother had insisted I wean myself from the sleeping pills, for Bear's sake if not mine. His jokes to break the tension and easy laughs were growing more seldom. That was about the time Sam started staying home more than he had ever during our married life.

I could tell that Sam, Bear and Mother were all worried about me, and I liked the feeling of knowing that Sam cared as well as the others. I had always been the caretaker in our family, but Sam had risen to the occasion when the worst happened.

By the time Sam had come home with the tickets, I had been off the pills a couple months and was beginning to sleep better. I was finally able to think about other things than all the "what ifs." Bear started making his jokes again and I could genuinely smile.

"Marion," said Sam, squeezing my hand again, "you *know* I don't mean to forget about William. We'll never forget about him. When I say forget the past, I mean forget the things we've said and done to hurt each other, to forget all that and start over."

He looked at me pleadingly, and as this was what I wanted almost more than anything in the world, I raised my glass again, and said, "To a new start. To today."

After we sealed the promise with a kiss, he said, "I have one more surprise for you."

"What?" The trip just for us, the change in Sam's attention to me, the surprises and romance, were filling my heart to the brim with fresh love and hope that things *could* be different. Sam reached into his inner jacket pocket and brought out a small gift box with a gold bow.

I looked at him in surprise. "Jewelry?" I unwrapped the bow and opened the lid. Inside were two earrings. Larger than I normally wear, their square stones were a brilliant brown.

"They reminded me of your eyes," said Sam. "They're called brown zircon." He watched to see my response and then continued. "I found them when I was on that business trip to Turkey. The jeweler told me that zircon has the power of protection, faith, beauty, love, honor, peace, and healing. I thought that perfectly represented our new start." He pointed to the box. "Look on the back…they're screw-ons. I told the jeweler you are kind of hard on earrings and usually lose them, so he suggested adding the screw-ons. Now you can put them on and never worry about them again."

I laughed with relief, because my first thought after how pretty and unusual they looked had actually been that I'd probably lose one of them before we made it back to the States. I quickly pulled off my inexpensive hoops and put on the new brown gems. I carefully screwed them in place and turned toward him for inspection.

"How do I look?"

"Even more beautiful," he said.

I stood up. "I'm going to the ladies' room to see what they look like," I said. Then I leaned back over Sam and kissed him again. "I love you. Thank you." I hurried towards the sign that said "LAVS" and followed the arrows downstairs.

In the lavatory, I glanced at myself in the mirror and smiled back at myself. The earrings were elegant, and they matched my chestnut-coloured eyes and hair, which I had to admit looked remarkably okay given the long flight. However, my face was starting to look pale and tired and my makeup was disappearing. I had left my handbag with my lipstick on the table, so I washed my hands and headed back up the stairs.

I turned the corner and stopped in confusion. Sam wasn't at our table and it had been wiped clear. I shook my head. Maybe I was disoriented from the jet lag and the table was behind me. I twirled around, ready to laugh at myself, but Sam was still nowhere to be seen. I walked to the table and sat down, looking under both chairs. My handbag was gone too.

Then, it occurred to me that Sam might have gone to the lav, too, and had taken my bag with him to make sure it was safe. I would wait there until he returned.

A different waitress came to the table. "Love, can I get you anything?"

Despite my anxiety, I was secretly pleased to hear her English accent. "No, thank you," I said, repeating the question under my breath.

I was ready to go back to the hotel and take the nap Sam had mentioned. I'd left my phone in my purse, so I had no way of telling the time or even looking at my pictures from the sites of the day to entertain myself while I waited. I had gotten my first smartphone after Wills told me I needed to move into the twenty-first century, and I had started to rely on it for everything.

At least ten minutes passed, and I began to worry. Maybe Sam was sick and was praying for me to come find him. I took a deep breath, got up, and walked back down the stairs, where I hesitated in front of the men's room. Having a husband and two sons for almost twenty years, there wasn't much that was going to shock me, so I pushed the door open and peered in. No one was there.

Now I was irritated. This was more like the old Sam, but I managed to push that negative thought down. He must have had a good reason to leave—I would just walk out of the pub and look for him. He was probably standing just outside waiting for me.

I hurried back upstairs, glanced around the pub once more, and then found the new waitress and asked for the bill.

"The bill?" she asked, squinting and then nodding her head. "Oh, yes, the *check*, love. It's been paid. You're all right."

I forgot Sam paid for our food and pints when he ordered at the bar. Did he leave a tip? Were you supposed to tip here? I would ask him when I found him, and I assumed he was outside.

I stepped out onto the sidewalk and glanced up and down the street. There were several gift shops filled with English and Scottish wares, so I hurriedly walked into each one. I could easily see that my tall, slim husband wasn't among the teapots, tea towels, or tea biscuits in any of them.

On the way to the pub, we had walked along the castle wall, so I retraced my steps and turned down the street where I'd stopped to look at a window display of floral china tea sets and Union Jack bunting. Just past the shop, I saw our lovely, romantic inn. Flowers climbed around the doorway and encircled the sign dated 1786.

I walked through the lobby past the fireplace flickering with candles and went straight upstairs to our first-floor room. When Sam and I had arrived earlier, I had giggled at my confusion when the desk clerk called the lobby "the reception" and said our room was "upstairs" on the first floor.

This time, though, I didn't giggle. My room key was in my purse, which Sam had with him. After knocking a couple of times, I pounded on the door. "Hello! Sam, open up!"

When I heard no sounds from inside the room, I went back down to the front desk and asked them to let me in. At least I could rest in the room until he turned up. A young man in a three-piece navy suit was manning the front desk.

"May I help you, Madam?" he said in his brilliant British accent.

I nodded. "Yes, please. I'm Marion Martin. My husband Sam has my room key, and I need to get into our room."

"Of course," he replied. "Which room are you in? What is your surname again?"

"We are in number twelve, and my last name is Martin."

I waited while he typed on his computer and took the opportunity to practice patience. I stared at his thin-striped tie and the silk polka-dotted handkerchief peeping out of his coat pocket and wondered if I could ever get Sam to wear something so polished.

The young man continued to type and finally shook his head. "I'm sorry, Madam. What room and name did you say?"

I thought perhaps that he hadn't understood my American accent, so I repeated slowly, "We are in number twelve." I held up my one finger, then two fingers. "And my surname is Martin. M-A-R-T-I-N."

He shrugged his shoulders. "I'm sorry, Madam, I do not have the name Martin in our system. Did you perhaps make the reservation under a different name or for a different day?"

Now impatient, I shook my head. "No, no, I'm *not* checking in. My husband, Sam Martin, and I already checked in a few hours ago. We've already put our luggage in the room. We left to get lunch, and then my husband—who has my room key—and I got separated in town. He'll come back here, but we've already checked in."

The young man excused himself and returned with an older gentleman, similarly dressed, whose name plate stated that he was the manager. "I'm sorry, Madam, but we have no record of you or your husband checking in today. Do you have your passport?"

I had done nothing wrong, but I felt guilty. "No, I don't have my passport or any ID with me. My husband has all that with him."

"Perhaps you have the wrong hotel. From where did you come?"

I looked around at the lobby at the same flower arrangements, the same red armchairs, the same gold mirror, and the same front desk. "We flew in today from the U.S. This is the Windsor Inn, right?"

"Yes, it is," the men answered in unison.

The older man cleared his throat. "Perhaps you have a room at the Windsor *House* or the Windsor *Gardens* or the—"

"No, I was just here this morning." I tried to remain calm. "A woman was here—she had dark blonde hair and a Polish accent."

The men glanced at one another, and the manager said, "Our colleague has gone home for the day. She will not be back to work until tomorrow."

"Can you please just let me look in the room?" I wanted to add that they probably thought I was a stupid American, and that I was smart enough to know which hotel I was staying at, but I stopped myself. I was frustrated now, and their politeness was irking me.

The manager smiled and nodded. "Yes, Madam, as there is no one staying in Number Twelve, we can go up together and take a look and see if there has been a mistake on our part."

"Thank you," I said through clenched teeth. "That would be lovely."

I followed him up the flight of stairs and he slid the magnetic key through the lock and stepped aside. "After you, please, Madam."

"Thank you," I said and walked inside.

Our suitcases were gone. My jacket was gone. I hurried to the bathroom, but my toiletry bag was gone. I could feel tears coming to my eyes. "I don't understand," I said.

The manager opened the door. "Madam, I think you can see now that you were mistaken and that you must have checked into a hotel with a similar name or location. There are many here in Windsor and it can be confusing for someone unfamiliar. May I call a taxi for you to try a different place?"

I shook my head. "All my money is in my handbag." I swallowed hard, trying to keep calm and compose myself. "I'll leave now and look for my husband," I said. "This is just some simple mistake."

"Yes, I'm sure it is," said the manager. He held the door open for me and I was crossing the threshold when a ringing sound, like that of an old house phone, began. A red cell phone I had not noticed before lay on the edge of the duvet.

I hurried back into the room but the manager got to it first. "Hello," he said, and after listening for a moment, he turned to me with a quizzical expression. "It's for you. The caller is asking for Marion."

I grabbed the phone from his hand. "Hello? Sam?"

"Marion," said a computerized female voice, "do exactly what you are told, and you will see Sam again."

I swallowed hard. "What?" The strange message was repeated.

"What do you want me to do?"

"A cab is waiting in front of the hotel for you. Get into it. Don't say anything to anyone."

I could feel my voice shaking. "Let me speak to Sam."

"Do exactly what you are told, and you will see Sam again," said the voice, and the call ended.

2

A Very Long Day

My stomach lurched, and I felt nauseous. I looked at the manager, who was now staring back at me. Still holding the phone in my hand, I walked out of the room, down the stairs, and out the door of the hotel. The window of a black cab parked in front of the hotel was rolled down and a hand waved at me to get in.

What are you doing? I thought. *No nurse or mother would get in a suspicious car with a stranger.* I ran back inside and gasped at the two suited men at the desk. "Call the police! Call the police! Something's happened to my husband! Hurry!"

The red phone in my hand rang again. "Marion," the computer voice intoned, "if you talk to the police or to anyone, then you will not see Sam again."

The men looked at me in confusion. "Never mind," I said. And squeezing back tears, I walked back out of the hotel and got into the back seat of the cab.

I looked to the left side of the front seat to see who was driving but no one was there. Then the cab moved into the left lane and I jerked in even more fright until I remembered that I was in England.

Earlier in the day, I would have taken a picture of the cab, the driver, and the street with glee, but now I squeezed the handle in fear. "Where's Sam? Where's my husband? What's going on?"

All I could see of the driver was a blonde ponytail. I looked in the rearview mirror and realized I'd seen her face before. "You're the waitress from the pub. Is this a joke? What's going on? Where's Sam?"

The woman turned slightly towards the mirror and looked at me, but she was no more talkative than she'd been at the pub. She turned left into what seemed to be oncoming traffic, and I flinched, instinctively dodging the cars with my body. "Where are you taking me? Please tell me where Sam is!"

Still no answer. After another minute, she turned into a car park and pulled into a space. Before I could react, the back door on the side opposite me opened, and a second woman got into the car. She was slim with long legs and dressed in a black suit—trousers and a blazer. Although she wore dark sunglasses, I recognized her immediately. It was Blythe, a colleague of Sam's.

I breathed a sigh of relief. "Thank goodness it's you. I've been so worried about Sam. He disappeared and took my purse with him, so I didn't have any ID or money, and the hotel had no record of us checking in. Then this phone rang and told me to get in the cab."

I'd met Blythe only a few times. The last time I'd seen her was at William's funeral, and I thought she was nice to have traveled all the way to Ohio from New York to pay her respects.

I knew that she and Sam had worked together on international sales projects. They'd traveled together a lot and it had crossed my mind more than once that she saw him more than I did. Although she'd only ever been polite to me, I'd always been slightly resentful of her. My mother, too, had made insinuating comments about the two of them.

Blythe turned to look at me, but I couldn't see her eyes. She wasn't smiling and I was unnerved. "Marion," she said, hesitating. "How to tell you this?"

My stomach twisted, and my hands started shaking. She was coming to tell me bad news about Sam, that he'd gotten sick or something, but why *she* was telling me and why she was doing it in a mysterious cab didn't make sense.

I squeaked out a response. "Just tell me." I just wanted to get the bad news over with. All news over the last year had been bad: William, my mom's health and accusations, Sam and me fighting over whose fault everything was. "If you can't say something nice, then don't say anything at all" had seemed to be our modus operandum.

I repeated the question. "Where's Sam?"

Blythe spoke in a monotone. "Sam is in jail."

"For what? What do you mean? What's wrong?"

She sighed and began speaking again. "Marion, Sam is in jail to keep him safely in custody so I can keep an eye on him. He has something of mine. You can say he stole it from me, so it's appropriate he is in jail. Once he tells where my possession is, he can go free."

She lowered her sunglasses slightly and widened her eyes at me. "Sam and I have always had a good working relationship. I'm not sure what you thought we were doing together on all those overseas assignments, but we quite enjoyed our work together."

I couldn't say anything. My mother had told me time and time again that Sam's job was suspicious and that his colleague was too.

Blythe continued. "It seems you were content to turn a blind eye and let the bills be paid and to take care of those fine sons of yours." I bristled at the mention of the boys, especially since she was beginning to sound like Mom. She glanced away and then back at me. "Sam changed the last year, of course, after what happened to

18

William, and he wanted to spend more time at home with his family. Those are all honourable intentions if you are the forgiving type, but before he left on this romantic attempt at a holiday with you, he took something that belongs to me. And I want it back."

I twisted uncomfortably on the back seat. "What did he take?" I whispered. "Where is the jail? I need to talk to him." The ponytail in front of me swayed as the driver shifted. "And what about her? Is she an undercover policewoman? Is that why she was at the pub? To arrest Sam?"

Blythe laughed, but it was clear her attempt at humor was fake. "You could say she's an undercover officer. That's one way of putting it. Sam is in jail so that he understands perfectly that I can make things happen. I can have him arrested. I can make a hotel think you never existed. I can make you obey the instructions on a strange phone and get in a cab."

She slid her sunglasses back up and turned to the front. "I will give you twenty-four hours to think about how you can encourage Sam to give me back what is mine, and then I will let you talk to him. Once you convince him to return my property and it is properly back in my possession, then I will leave you both alone to return to your pathetic life of lies. However, if you go to the police to look for him before that, I will make more things happen, and they won't be pleasant."

I wasn't sure I understood what she was saying. "In twenty-four hours, you want me to do what? What about Sam?"

"*Your* job is to remain quiet. I will contact you at the appropriate time to see if you are ready to help Sam tell the truth. He, on the other hand, has twenty-four hours to decide if he is willing to tell *me* the truth." She gestured toward the door on my side of the car. "It's time for you to go now. I will contact you tomorrow. Remember, do not go to the police on your own and do not contact anyone about this. I will be watching." She leaned over and tapped the red phone that was still in my hand.

I clutched the phone with numb fingers and opened the door. As I slid out, she called out to me once more. "I'll be watching. Wait for the call."

The cab glided into reverse and sped out of the car park, leaving me standing in the middle of a town in a foreign country where I knew no one, had no ID or money, and had no place to go. Terrified, I glanced around at people walking about and wondered if they were watching me.

Finally, I headed for the sidewalk. *Just walk, Marion,* I told myself. *Just keep walking.*

3

Coffee and Castles

My random steps led me toward the Thames River where I could see families throwing bread crumbs to swans straining their long white necks over one another to reach the food.

That's what I'd thought I'd be doing on this trip—romantically walking along the Thames feeding swans—but instead Sam had disappeared, Blythe was threatening me, and I didn't know what to do.

Normally, I would have called my mother or a friend to ask what they thought I should do. Check that. *Normally*, I would have gone to the police in an emergency. But this was definitely not normal. My heart was racing, and my eyes and head ached from being awake for way too long and the stress of what was happening. *Should I just find a place to sit and wait until the phone rang again? Should I ignore Blythe and go to the police and see Sam?*

That's when it occurred to me that I could sneak to the jail and see him. I was his wife, after all, so surely the police would let me see him and then I could ask him what was going on.

As I hesitated in anguish amongst people boating, strolling babies, talking and laughing, I noticed an older white-haired man walking toward me. He was dressed in a Harris-tweed cap and holding a long black umbrella, and had a brown and white spaniel prancing on a lead. If he had a dog with him, I guessed, he was more likely to be a local than a tourist. I put my hand up to catch his attention.

"Excuse me, do you know where the police department is?"

He stopped abruptly, and his dog sat and looked up at his master.

"The Thames Valley Police?"

"Is that what it's called here? Yes, where is that?"

He paused. I wondered if he was Blythe's spy, but the man was thinking of the best way to explain how to get there. "It's on a side road just down this way," he said, pointing behind him. "Bear right at the mews and then when you see—"

I interrupted him. "I'm really sorry, but I don't know what a mews is. Can you say that again, please?" Although I loved his accent, the strain of listening to it and an unfamiliar term was too much for me.

"Here." He touched his cap and held out his umbrella in a grand gesture. "I'll show you the way."

I was terrified that this was a trick and the man would take me straight to Blythe, but I couldn't think of what else to do. "All right," I said. "Thank you."

"Come on, Charlie, let's take this young lady to TVP," said my guide to the spaniel, who thumped his tail in response.

The gentleman walked away from the river, and I kept pace with him. We walked in silence a few steps, then he asked in proper British, "From where are you? Canada? I hear an accent."

"No, the United States. Ohio."

"Ah, America. I've been to the States before," he said. "Busy place. I was in Los Angeles. Quite warm."

"Yes, yes, it *is* warm there," I replied, but I wanted him to walk faster and not talk. I needed to think.

We reached a cobblestone alley with a sign on the building that read Windsor Mews and he turned to walk that way. At least, I knew now that a mews was some sort of street. The gentleman bent down to unclip the lead from the dog's collar and kept walking without turning once to look back at Charlie, who stopped to sniff at a container in front of a door. Pink roses filled the container and climbed up a trellis that graced the doorway. Each door on the cobblestone alleyway was graced in front with potted flowers and a small table with chairs just perfect for an afternoon tea break.

We kept walking and Charlie hustled along the cobblestones to catch up with us. The man glanced at me. "Is this an emergency? Because I can call the police on my mobile if you need me to."

"No. Thank you very much, but I need to go in person to the station."

He glanced up high to a building that stood above the alley. "In the days of horses and carriages, that building used to be one large mansion for a wealthy family. The mews was the back where the horses were kept. These small houses we are walking by were once barns for the horses and birds. Stable boys lived back here." He shook his head. "Now these little houses sell for over a million pounds. What a day."

"Yes, what a day," I said. *What an understatement*, I thought. "Are we close?"

We walked to the end of the mews to a new street and turned right. He pointed to an inn covered in hanging baskets and window boxes of colorful flowers. "That is the Castle Inn. When you pass it, turn left, and you will see the TVP station."

I thanked him and waved as the gentleman reversed course. As soon as he and his dog were out of sight, I started to run.

When I reached the building that housed the police, I tried to open the door, but it was locked. I looked for a call button or buzzer, but I didn't see anything, so I knocked louder and harder. Still no one came. I glanced at the sign and realized that the station had closed at 5:00. *What kind of a police station was this?*

The sign said to call 999 if it was a life-threatening emergency, but there was no way to call out on the red phone. I would have to find a place to spend the night and then come back to the station when it opened. I longed to see Sam and talk to him, assuming that Blythe hadn't lied to me. But I would have to come back in the morning at eight.

I had no money, no toothbrush, nothing. I berated myself for even coming on the trip and leaving Bear with my mom. *What kind of woman leaves her handbag at the table and doesn't take it with her?*

I walked back in the direction of the pub where Sam and I had had lunch and saw a sign pointing to the Long Walk. I knew there was a park in front of Windsor Castle, so I followed the arrow and came upon a beautiful stretch of green lawn and a pavement that started at the iron gates in front of the castle and went straight ahead and out of sight.

Couples strolled along arm-in-arm and numerous dogs chased balls. I sat, leaning against a big tree that was probably hundreds of years old, and as much as my mind was racing, I couldn't stop my eyes from closing.

I woke with a jerk from a dream that Charlie the dog was barking good-bye at me, and an angry lady with a long blonde ponytail was running towards me. A dog, but not Charlie, was nuzzling me.

"Merlin, come back here," called the woman, and the miniature black poodle raced off back to his mistress. I wiped my mouth and sat up straighter, looking around to see if Blythe or her driver were in sight. Locals jogged by me, but no one looked familiar. I had no idea how much time had passed. I scolded myself again for leaving my bag on the table and for coming at all.

Bear was staying with my mother for a few days until his university orientation began and he moved into a dorm. On the last week of our trip, he was supposed to start the fall semester. All the other freshman parents would be driving their children to school, helping them move into their dorms, and meeting their children's roommates. But *I* had selfishly flown off across the ocean to chase the dream of a happy marriage and left my youngest—and now only—child. The child is supposed to leave and make an empty nest—not the parents.

But Sam's holiday plans for six weeks abroad sounded good at the time. Even my mother seemed happy we were going on a trip together.

"I'll make sure Bear is packed and well-fed his last week at home, and I'll go with him to move him in. It will be fun for us and distracting. Marion, you go and have fun and don't worry about us," she said.

Bear chimed in. "Mom, Gramma's right." He leaned down and wrapped me in a big hug. My younger son always laughed a lot, loved teasing his more studious older brother, and always tried to make jokes to keep the peace between his father and me.

Sam and I had gotten Bear a laptop for his high school graduation present, and our plan was to do video calls with him once he was settled at school. The campus was only an hour away from home, and my mother's was even closer to him. I wished I could see him—the fuzzy brown hair that he wore too long, his tan from life-guarding during the summer, and his light brown eyes that almost close when he laughs.

I imagined that he would be awake by now—Mom was probably making him bacon and pancakes doused with butter and honey.

The sound of a crying toddler snapped me out of my whiny thoughts. It was getting to be completely dark, and I thought I probably shouldn't stay out in the open, as I didn't know who was watching me. My legs and back were cramped, so I stood and stretched before walking back towards the lights of the town. I needed to find a place to spend the night—or hide. It was colder now, and I wished I had one of the sweaters I had so carefully packed.

I followed the signs back along the high street to the train station Sam and I had ridden on from London to Windsor that morning. It now seemed ages ago. The once bustling shops and cafes were all closed—the only places still open were nice restaurants, and I had no money to go inside one of those. I could see diners sitting on outdoor terraces under heating lamps. One restaurant appeared to provide blankets for their outdoor patrons, and I envied the Scottish plaids wrapped warmly around them.

Then I had an idea. What if I rode on the *train* for warmth and to rest? The thought of sitting down on a real seat sounded lovely, so I hurried to the platform. Sam and I had even taken pictures of the train we'd ridden into Windsor. I still had the ticket stub in my pocket—I'd kept it as a souvenir. We had no trains in Ohio, and the novelty of it had been fun. Now being safe and warm seemed fun.

I looked around. There wasn't a ticket turnstile at the station, but I might need to show my ticket on the train. *What would the train conductor do to me if he caught me? Take me to jail?* I hoped so, because that was where I wanted to be anyway.

I boarded the next train and sank into a seat, leaning my head against the window. I felt more normal rather than homeless, and I could think again.

I needed to go over in my mind what had happened again. One. At the pub, I'd gone downstairs to the lav, and when I had gotten back, Sam and all our belongings were gone. Two. There was no record of us at the hotel. Three. A red phone was on the bed and Blythe, in a computer voice, had called on it.

I put my hand in my pocket and felt the phone still there. I pulled it out to inspect it more closely. As I said, there was no way to call out on it. It didn't have internet or other "smart" features, but I'd seen enough spy movies to know that Blythe could probably see me somehow or that the phone had a tracking device on it. Before I could safely go to the police and see Sam, I had to get rid of it. When I got off the train at the next station, I would leave the phone behind.

The next station was Slough. The track ended there, and everyone on the train started getting off. No conductor had come by to check tickets, so I hadn't been arrested yet. "All change here," said the announcer said in her lovely voice. "This stop is Slough." She pronounced the name like it rhymed with "cow" and I shook my head—I would have guessed it rhymed with "rough."

I snapped myself back to attention. No matter how it was pronounced, I didn't want to get arrested in Slough, so I got off the train. I saw exits around the corner and knew I would have to use my ticket to exit the station. The whistle blew, which meant the train was about to leave again, and I changed tactics midstream. I laid the phone down on a bench in the station and got back on the train.

I felt better already. I would ride the train back to Windsor. In the morning, I could go to the police without being tracked.

When the train pulled into the Windsor station, I got off with a handful of passengers. My plan was to go back down to the Thames, find a place to sit and rest, and then keep moving until morning.

As I walked toward the station exit, I heard a phone ringing and looked in the direction of the noise. The red phone lay on an empty café table behind me! I stared at it for a moment. It was ringing and ringing, but there was no one near it. My heart was pounding, but I picked it up and held it up to my ear. The female computer voice was back. "Did you forget something? Maybe you don't remember what I told you or perhaps you think I wasn't serious. Wait until I call you with instructions and do NOT go to the police. I AM serious. Sam, tell Marion how serious I am."

I yelled into the phone. "Sam, help me! Are you there? What's happening?"

There was silence, and then I heard my husband's voice. "Marion, are you all right?"

"Yes," I whispered this time, "I'm okay, but what's happening? Where are you?"

"I'm really sorry, Marion. Really. I'll explain everything tomorrow. Just do what Blythe says and find a place to wait until she contacts you. Everything will be fine."

We were interrupted by the annoying computer voice. "Yes, Marion, everything will be fine. *If* Sam hands over what belongs to me." The phone clicked, and I was alone again.

I didn't know if I felt better or worse. Sam was alive, so that was good, but if he was with Blythe, didn't that mean he wasn't in jail? Why wouldn't he just give Blythe back whatever is was so we could go on and just try to forget everything that had happened—go back to our "life of lies," as Blythe had called it?

What could Sam have of hers? Some memento from their relationship? Now that Sam was acting more like a husband and father, was she resentful? For that, would she have had Sam arrested or kidnapped or take my purse and suitcase? Thoughts were racing through my mind.

Maybe it was something to do with their job. Sam was in international sales for a technology company and he had explained things about it off and on over the years, but I hadn't really paid attention to exactly what he did. He went to work, often for weeks at a time overseas, and I did my job as a nurse and took care of the boys.

The old feelings of resentment and blame started bubbling up in me again, but I pushed them back down. Blythe obviously wanted to scare me, and so far, she had been successful.

I would have to figure it all out later. Sam was in trouble, and I needed to find a place to spend the night. I was getting colder and there were almost no people walking around the station. Cleaners were sweeping the platform and a man in uniform was locking one of the gates to the station. I needed to leave.

I thought about bedding down with the swans, but then I remembered how they bit each other over food and thought better of it. I could just keep walking around and sitting on benches, but hiding in a warm, well-lit place seemed safer. I hadn't really paid attention to the crime rate when I had done my travel research, but my instincts seemed to say to get inside.

What do homeless people in England do? I wondered. Maybe there was a shelter and I could even ask there to contact the police. But how could I find out where a shelter was without asking someone? It didn't seem wise to announce to a stranger that I was homeless. Not that I had anything to steal except for the red phone.

Windsor Castle towered above the high grey stone wall that surrounded the castle and its property. Lights beamed from its windows in contrast with the darkening town around me. The queen owned all those swans swimming and biting in the Thames. Maybe *she* could take me in for the night. I imagined how much fun it would be to have a slumber party with Queenie, and then realized I probably felt more like the peasants in the older days: hungry, tired, and cold, and stuck outside the castle walls while knights feasted and roaring fires blazed inside.

I walked back down the high street following the castle wall and noticed the Guildhall. It looked sort of like a church, but I knew from my pre-trip research and planning that it was the city hall where Prince Charles and Camilla were married. Since they had each been married before—and divorced—they couldn't get married in the Church of England.

When I got closer, I saw that it was locked up for the night. Then I noticed a picturesque hundreds-of-years-old stone church tucked in amongst the side buildings—just the sort of medieval site I would have happily taken a picture of just a few hours before.

Lights shone through the stained-glass windows, and I could hear singing. I walked up to the heavy wooden doors and pulled on one of them. I could hear the singing voices much more clearly—about a dozen older men and ladies were singing an old hymn, led by a choir director in a tweed jacket and scruffy trousers. A tiny ancient woman played the organ. She looked too fragile to play yet she pumped the pedals and keys with both hands and feet with aplomb.

The singers didn't seem to notice me. The director had his back to me, and the organist was fully engaged in her mammoth task.

"When I survey the wondrous Cross
On which the Prince of Glory died,
My richest gain I count but loss,
And pour contempt on all my pride."

I made a quick decision that this was where I was going to stay the night and looked around for a place to hide. After all, a church is supposed to be a place of refuge, a safe haven, and I needed both.

There were wooden pews all along the floor leading up to the choir, but they were too narrow to hide under or on without being seen. Then I noticed a table near me in the foyer, set up with tall posters displaying notice of a family picnic. The table was draped with a tapestry that went all the way to the floor. I glanced at the choir again, but they were still passionately singing.

Love so amazing, so divine,
Demands my Soul, my Life, my All.

I crouched down, trying to keep my body lower than the pews and crept towards the table. I lifted the cloth and saw cardboard boxes underneath. As quietly as I could, I pushed the boxes out on the back side of the table. Once the boxes were out of the way, I crawled under the table and made sure all of me was covered by the tablecloth. My heart was racing, and resentment swelled up in me at Sam for putting me in the terrifying predicament of hiding from elderly people in church.

Finally, the music stopped, and I heard a man say, "Ladies and gentlemen and Noel." Laughter echoed through the cavernous church. The director continued. "That last time sounded loverly. We are almost ready for our performance for Sunday's evensong. We will meet twice more before then to run through our songs again. Now should we wet our whistles down the street?"

There were general sounds of affirmation and acquiescence. Murmuring voices, like children being let out for recess, came closer to the front of the church door—and closer to me. But no one seemed to be leaving, and my legs were cramping from the effort of keeping them tucked under me and out of sight. One lady's voice stood out. "Angela, I thought I saw a woman come in the front door whilst we were singing the last song. Did you see her?"

I mimicked her pronunciation of "Angeler" and "whilst" under my breath, and then scolded myself. I was going to get caught like a child being held in for recess who's supposed to keep quiet.

"No, I didn't notice anyone," said Angela, apparently. "Why? Do you think she's still here?"

"I don't see anyone now, but I'm sure I noticed someone come in. She had brown hair and was wearing a red coat."

Inwardly, I regretted wearing such a bright red color, but I had bought it because I thought it would look so nice in all the pictures I'd planned to take of our trip. Now it was making me look like Little Red Riding Hood just when I needed to hide from the wolf.

The director's voice boomed. "All right, everyone, let's take our conversation down to the Victoria. A pint will help all our voices and I need to lock up." I heard more laughs and talking as the group of singers began exiting.

Just as the door shut, the red phone rang. I flipped it open and whispered "Hello," but there was no voice this time. I froze as I heard the door open again and a man's voice call out to someone outside. "Someone's mobile rang. They'll be wanting that before the morning. I'll meet you there."

I listened intently to his footsteps as he walked through the narthex and up the nave. I squeezed the phone as hard as I could and willed it not to make a sound. I wasn't sure if hiding in a church was against the law here, but it probably was.

The man's humming came closer to my hiding spot under the table, and I thought this was an appropriate place to *pray* with all my heart for the phone not to ring. My prayer apparently worked, and I breathed a sigh of relief when I heard the heavy wooden door open and close and the sound of a lock clicking. Better to be locked *in* church than out.

I waited to be sure they were gone and decided to sleep under the table in case there was a night watchman or cameras. Sam had told me there were CCTVs everywhere in England, but I didn't know if that meant churches, too. *Were the church and state separate in this country or was that just in America?* The name Church of England seemed to blend the two.

Then it occurred to me that if I was on camera and arrested, I would be in jail with Sam. And even being in jail and not homeless and hungry sounded better than sleeping on a cold hard floor under a table with a growling, empty stomach.

A hopeful thought came to me that once I went to the police station in the morning, they could look at the cameras at the pub and find out what happened to Sam. If the police couldn't help me, my next plan was to locate the American Embassy. Isn't helping an American citizen find her missing husband what we've been paying our taxes for all this time?

All I knew was that I didn't trust Blythe. I curled up on my side and used one of the boxes as a pillow. The earrings that Sam had given me pressed into the side of my head, but from sheer bodily exhaustion, I fell asleep to dream about phones ringing, cars crashing in the rain, and an organist pounding.

I woke up a few hours later with a terrible taste in my mouth and a pain in my stomach from hunger, but I felt better seeing the bit of sunlight flooding in through the stained-glass windows. It was actually quite lovely, or should I say "loverly," to see the colours streaming into the foyer. Sunshine meant a new day. Surely it was a sign, after yesterday's overcast greyness, that today all the mysteries would be resolved.

I crawled out from under the table and pushed the boxes back under. I gazed around at the cathedral ceiling and beautiful artwork and tapestries and felt peace that today everything would be better. Sam would give Blythe whatever it was she wanted, and we'd finish our trip. Or maybe we'd just go back home. Suddenly, being an Ohio soccer mom who watched the Travel Channel didn't seem so mundane anymore.

I decided I should pray one more time for help since it had worked the night before. "Oh, God," I whispered, "thank you for sharing your house with me and giving me a safe place to sleep. Please help me find Sam and get this all worked out."

I tried to open the church door, but it wouldn't budge no matter how hard I pushed and pulled. There was a massive key hole, and I figured there must be a giant key around somewhere. I started to look around for one but decided to crawl back under my table of refuge until people began arriving. The historic church was a tourist destination, so I thought once a crowd formed, I would come out, blend in, and slip out.

Before I could make it back to the table, though, I heard someone fumbling at the lock. I ran as fast I could towards the back of the church and ducked behind the altar. My heart was hammering again. *Was it the police? A cleaning crew? Perhaps it was someone coming to the altar to pray.* I heard humming similar to that of the previous night and assumed that the choir director had returned. I touched the red phone in my pocket and prayed once more that it would stay silent until I managed to escape.

The footsteps echoed all over the sanctuary until finally I heard a door slam shut and the humming cease. I waited another minute and then dashed irreverently down the nave and out the front door. As I walked quickly down the steps and away, the phone emitted its now familiar ring. *That was a close call*, I thought, rolling my eyes at my own pun. "Hello? Sam?"

My hopeful question was met by the same mechanical female voice. "Marion, I trust you had a good night's sleep and will now be prepared to help persuade Sam to do the right thing."

"Is Sam OK? Can I speak to him?" I gripped the phone tightly and waited.

"Sam is alive, but he is not making good decisions. He has a few more hours to return the stolen property or there will be significant consequences. Be at the car park where we met yesterday at half past two." Before I could speak, the connection ended.

I stared at the phone and held it to my ear again, but no one was there. Blythe's threat convinced me she meant business. I just wanted Sam to give her back what she wanted and get back to me. I choked a bit and tears welled up in my eyes. *Wasn't there enough trauma in our small family already?*

An enormous growl from my stomach brought me back to the present. I deliberately focused on something my mother told me often after Wills' death. "Don't dwell on yesterday. Avoid thinking about tomorrow. Focus on the day *before* tomorrow. You can manage today," I could hear her say. I straightened my shoulders. I needed to make it until 2:30 p.m. and pray that Sam made it, too.

The bell from the church started ringing the hour. I kept count and heard seven bongs of the bell. That meant the police station opened in an hour. *Should I try to find Sam, or as Blythe had commanded, avoid the police?*

I carefully looked for traffic approaching from the right and crossed the street, continuing into a pedestrian-only shopping area. It seemed only coffee shops were open so early. I thought how charmed I would have been if I were there on vacation like I was supposed to be.

I watched as a homeless man asked people headed to work for

spare change. First, he apologized and then thanked them whether they dropped a few coins in his cup or not. Before I could even think, I turned towards a man in a business suit who was passing by me, and in my best British accent said, "Spare any change, sir?"

The man barely looked at me as he dropped coins into my outstretched hand. "Cheers," he mumbled, hurrying on.

I was astonished. "Thank you, sir," I said.

I looked down at the handful of foreign coins and carefully counted the amount stamped on each one, wondering if I had enough for a baguette at one of the coffee shops. I leaned up against a store front and continued to ask for donations. Two men in suits kept walking, and like the homeless man I'd observed, I made sure to follow proper protocol and thank them sincerely.

The next couple of pedestrians were more generous. When I had enough for a cup of coffee, too, I went into a small café and walked to the loo to freshen up. My makeup was long gone and my hair was ratty, but the soap and water felt wonderful.

I stepped up to the counter to order a latte and baguette with butter and jam. I hoped they had tons of calories—to make up for my missing dinner and sleep the previous night.

"Name please, madam?" said the tattooed young man with multiple earrings in each ear.

"Marion," I replied with a smile.

The young man squinted at me. "Sorry. Did you say Mary?"

When that happens, I usually say "Marion, as in Marion, Ohio," but I doubted he would know about that small town. I tried my second-best explanation.

"Marion as in *Maid* Marion." If he didn't know who Robin Hood's girlfriend was, I would just be Mary.

"Ah, Maid Marion. All right. That will be two pound sixty." The simple act of interacting with someone who couldn't understand my diction made me feel completely human again.

I looked down at my coins hoping they added up to enough, attempted to count, and then finally held them out to him. He carefully counted the coins and took the amount from my hand.

"Canadian?"

I started to say that I was an American, just as I had to tell Charlie the dog's owner, but I thought better of it. Who knew who was with Blythe and spying or tracking me?

"Eh, yes, true. I'm a Canuck."

"I thought so," he said. "Cheers."

Sitting at the little café table, sipping my warm coffee and savoring every bite of the best bread I'd ever tasted, I felt normal again. After a few more minutes, I could think somewhat clearly. Sam had told me to wait for him, so I didn't think he wanted me to go to the police. I wanted to trust him, but what if he had a gun to his head and couldn't communicate to me what he really wanted?

The phone made a beeping sound and I quickly opened it, but it was a warning beep that the battery was about to die. What could I do? The phone was my lifeline to Sam.

I went back to the counter and asked in my best Canadian if there was a mobile charger I could borrow. The young man who had taken my order nodded. "Give me your mobile, Madam, and I'll charge it for you behind the counter."

"Thanks," I said and handed it over. I was all out of Canadian words at that point.

As I waited for the phone to charge, I noticed two teenaged girls dressed in smart burgundy and navy school uniforms who were sipping tea and typing away on their smartphones. I sat down beside them and smiled in my best mom way.

"Hiya, my mobile is dead and is charging. I need to post a message to my son, so he knows I'll be late to pick him up. Would either of you let me borrow your mobile for just a sec to do that?"

The girls looked at each other. One shrugged and handed me her phone.

"Thank you very much. Cheers." I quickly logged onto my Facebook account and saw the latest picture I had posted. It was a picture of Sam and me on the plane with the message, "On the way to the trip of a lifetime." I was pretty certain this was going to be my *last* trip of a lifetime.

I searched for my friend Freya's profile page and started writing her a private message. Although my old college roommate lived in Bath, several hours away, maybe she could come pick me up and let me borrow some money—or even help me with the police. Someone else knowing what was going on with Sam and me would be a relief. I didn't want to give too much information because I didn't want Sam to look bad, so I told her that I was in Windsor and had lost my purse and phone. I posted the message on her timeline hoping she would see it immediately.

I thanked the girls and returned the phone. As they got up giggling and left the cafe, my thoughts drifted back to Wills' memorial service. It seemed like the entire high school came, and even though there were tears all day long, the kids kept coming to talk to me about Wills and told stories that I hadn't heard. The kids made "memory books" for our family and brought balloons with special messages written on them to give us to make a huge bouquet.

It was a celebration of a life well lived. One of the best memories of the day was how Sam, who was typically absent at church or social events, stayed by my side, handing me tissues, hugging me, and sharing laughter at some of the memories Wills' friends shared.

I stayed at the café as long as I dared, but the lack of sleep and continued jet lag was overpowering. My new friend behind the counter finally told me my mobile was charged. I couldn't think of any reason to stay there without any money and I was afraid I would nod off.

As I walked outside, the sound of a loud band began. Looking towards the castle, I noticed the streets were cordoned off. British guards in their distinctive red uniforms and tall black bearskin hats were on every corner, guiding pedestrians off the streets and onto the pavement. A parade of similarly suited soldiers with brass instruments and drums began marching down the High Street. It was the Changing of the Guard! I hadn't known this happened at Windsor—I thought it was only at Buckingham Castle. Excited, I wished I had my real phone to take a video.

Across the street, I noticed the backs of two tall slim women with high blonde ponytails. I was really starting to hate the hairstyle. I was dressed in a red coat, just like the band, so I began marching alongside them, keeping time with their long strides by sheer determination. I turned slightly away from the opposite side of the street and tried not to bring attention to myself.

The band veered onto a side street and I veered with them. I took a chance and looked back—there were no blondies in sight. Just to be safe, I kept up with the soldiers until they reached a brick building with gates. There was another whistle and barking command, and the gates opened. The band began filing inside and I marched alongside them as far as I could go.

The buttered baguette from breakfast rumbled around in my stomach and I worried it might not stay down. Although I had harbored the idea that I still might go to the police, I decided then and there to avoid Blythe's unnecessary wrath, do as ordered and hide out until 2:30, when I was due to meet her at the car park.

I found a bench with overhanging foliage by the Thames where I could sit unobserved while I still had a good view of my surroundings. I watched the swans and alternated between fuming at Sam and wondering how I would know if Freya received my Facebook communication.

Finally, the church bells rang, followed by two chimes. I got up and walked as fast as I could toward the car park.

The street the car park was on was burned in my memory. I wasn't certain I liked knowing the town so well. I certainly wasn't doing the typical tourist route—I hadn't gone in the castle yet, but I knew where the jail was.

A Thames Valley Police Department car slowly rode past me. It was the first time I'd registered that they looked noticeably different from American police cars. The car was small with bright blue and yellow blocking and I wondered if Inspector Clouseau was inside.

I felt conspicuous in my red coat and noticed the police officer looking at me. Did he know I slept in the church last night or was begging for money this morning? Was it illegal to beg? I had no idea, but I knew it certainly wasn't socially accepted. I'd always assumed beggars were drug users or alcoholics, but this morning's experience had changed my perspective on poor people entirely. These were the most polite panhandlers I'd ever been around.

The police car slowed to a stop at the traffic light, and the officer continued to look at me. Did he know I was the American whose husband was locked up in his jail?

Before I could second-guess myself, I waved frantically at the policeman. I screamed and ran towards the car. "Help me! Wait!" The police lights flashed on and a man dressed in a neon-yellow vest that matched the outside of the car and a rounded black helmet got out of the car.

I ran across the street to him and the officer put his hand on his black baton—apparently in case he needed to protect himself from me. He didn't have a gun, and I wasn't sure if that made me feel more or less safe. *Wasn't it true that the police in England don't carry guns?*

The officer continued to rest his hand on his baton. "Yes, Madam, how may I help you?" The second officer in the car kept one hand on the steering column and two eyes on me. Just as I was about to respond with a plea for help, the phone in my hand started to ring. My stomach tightened in a knot. Blythe was watching from somewhere.

"Oh, sorry," I said in a British accent, "I needed directions, but now I remember which way to go." I hurried back across the street towards the car park, turning back around to see what reaction the officers had. They must have believed me—the car holding my hope drove off and out of my peripheral vision.

And the red phone kept ringing.

I glanced around looking at the tops of buildings. Maybe she was standing on the wall of Windsor Castle watching every move I made in the town below. More likely she was tracking me by satellite on the phone.

I opened the flip phone. "Sam?"

The computerized voice spoke. "Marion, since you are so determined to go to the police, just go to the station. Tell Sam to give me what is mine or neither of you will make it through the next twenty-four hours. Do you understand?"

I was terrified at her words, but I was relieved to go to the police rather than getting back in the black cab. On my list of one hundred worries was that she wouldn't ever let me *out* of the cab. Mafia movies of bodies thrown into rivers with bricks tied to their feet kept popping into my thoughts.

"Yes, I understand. I'm going right now."

"The last twenty-four hours, the two of you were separated, arrested, hungry and homeless. I can see your every move. I won't be so nice if you try to get rid of this phone again. Do you understand me?"

"Yes," I whispered.

"Twenty-four hours," repeated the voice, and I heard a click.

Clutching the phone, I ran down Windsor Mews towards the police station, stumbling over the uneven cobblestones. My side burned from the unusual exertion.

This time the station was busy with similarly-accoutered neon blue and yellow officers and cars. I reached for the door, but before I could open it, out walked an officer—with Blythe.

I froze. *Should I try to hide or scream for the man to arrest her for kidnapping?* Before I could do either, the black cab with the pony-tailed waitress pulled up and the officer opened the back door of the car. Blythe slid in and then looked directly at me. Glaring at me, she held up two fingers and then four. The cab drove away, and I heard the officer mumble. "Blasted boss. Thinks she can do anything." Then he looked at me. "Madam, can I help you?"

What? Blythe was his boss? She worked for the police? Did that mean that Sam worked for the police, too? I shook my head. "No, I mean, yes. I'm here to see my husband. Sam Martin."

The officer held the door open for me and looked at me as if memorizing what I looked like. "Mrs. Martin, your husband is being released right now. If you wait here, he will be out in a few minutes." He pointed to a small area by a front desk behind safety bars and mumbled to the man at the desk. "She's waiting here for a Mr. Martin to come out."

The officer sitting at the desk nodded to him and then looked at his computer screen and ignored me.

As I stood there waiting for my husband to get out of jail, my mind was racing with questions, worries, and fears. *What was really Sam's job and why was he arrested? Who was the bad guy? Was it Sam or Blythe? Or both?*

Every fear I'd had over the past years of marriage washed over me and I felt sick and weak. I had always pushed the thoughts of his long absences and relationships with colleagues away but now the innuendoes from Blythe and being homeless and penniless for a night and a day was just too much to push down anymore. I wanted the truth, and if I didn't like the answers, then I was ready to make a permanent change. Surely Freya would give me some money. Somehow, I'd get to the U.S. Embassy, get a new passport, and take a plane home and move in with my mother. She wouldn't be surprised.

A door opened with a loud buzz and Sam walked through. Unshaven, he looked tired, and I wanted to wrap my arms around his waist and hug him with relief, but I deliberately hardened myself to face the truth. He forced a smile and walked towards me. "Marion, I am really sorry. You must be scared and confused."

He reached out to take my hand, but I backed away. "Sam, I want to know what's going on. I'm not leaving this room until you tell me the truth."

The officer who had been sitting at the front desk immersed in his computer straightened up as if preparing for trouble about to happen. Sam glanced at the officer and then back at me. "Marion, let's walk outside where we can talk. I'll explain everything. I promise."

I wasn't sure what to do, but I didn't want either of us to get arrested for fighting in a police station, so I nodded yes and walked to the front door. Sam tried to open it for me, but I pushed ahead of him and walked out to show him that I didn't need him to take care of me. I had taken care of myself—albeit by possibly breaking some minor laws such as trespassing, loitering, hitchhiking a train, panhandling and lying to teenage girls and an officer of the law, but I was sure England would have some leniency since I was an American and was consequently a loud blundering idiot.

As soon as we walked outside into the gray, cooling air, I saw a black car and jumped, thinking it was Blythe's cab, but it was just a small black Smart car. I decided to walk closer to Sam after all. He reached his hand out again, and I let him take mine. He smiled reassuringly at me. "Let's get to where we can talk without being heard or seen."

Without saying another word, Sam herded me up and down streets and mews and sometimes the same street on the opposite side. I kept quiet, too. *What was there to say?* I wanted answers and hopefully, reassurance. I'd always been lulled by his false reassurances before. I told myself to stay on my guard.

We reached the square in front of the castle that overlooked the pedestrian-only shopping street. It was a market day and the street was lined with buskers, tent-covered boutiques of delightful wares, and yummy smelling foods, but I was either hiding from a deranged woman or blindly following a duplicitous man who happened to be my husband, so I couldn't really enjoy it all.

There were crowds of multi-national tourists. American men wore ball caps and khakis, and their wives wore comfortable but unfashionable walking sandals and capris. A tour group of Asians were taking pictures with selfie sticks and the castle in the background. There were at least two school groups dressed in dark uniforms comprised of blazers with trousers or skirts and dress shoes. Not a piercing or pastel hairdo in sight on these proper British students.

Sam seemed to relax once we were in the midst of the crowd, and he backed us up against a wall outside a busy coffee shop decorated with Union Jack flags and bunting. He scanned the people around us constantly.

"Can we talk?" I asked.

"Yes, for now," he said.

I had so many questions and wanted to understand what had happened over the last twenty-four hours. I was worried too about the next twenty-four hours, so my first really important question was, "Where's my purse? I didn't have any money or ID or anything." I could feel my voice getting teary and my eyes welling up.

"Marion, let me start at the beginning. Well, let me start with yesterday when you left me at the table to go look at your earrings." He pushed my hair back to see the earrings and smiled. "They do look really, really good with your hair."

I pushed his hand away. "Sam! Just tell me what happened!"

"Okay. You went downstairs, and that waitress you kept trying to talk to came up behind me at the table and pushed what felt like a gun into my back. She told me to come with her outside the pub, that her colleague was downstairs in the toilet with you, and that you would not be hurt if I did what she asked. I was so scared for you that I got up and went with her. She told me to get your purse and then we walked outside. A black cab was parked out front and she told me to get in the back seat. She took your purse and I never saw it again. I imagine she and Blythe are keeping it to analyze you."

I didn't know what he meant about their analyzing me, and I felt like he was holding back lots of details, but I didn't interrupt, and he kept talking. "Blythe, as I'm sure you can guess, was in the back seat of the car. While the driver, who I recognized as the woman who checked us into our hotel that morning, sat in the front seat pointing another gun at me. Blythe asked me where a certain item was that she and I procured on our last job together. It had been in her possession, but I secretly took it from her. She obviously figured that out and wants it back. I can't explain to you yet what it is. You have to trust me."

"But if it's hers, isn't that stealing, and isn't that why she had you arrested?"

The crowd around us thinned out significantly as the school group of uniformed teenagers and the Asian tour group disappeared into the ticket office. Sam took my hand again. "It's a little more complicated than that. Let's go inside the ticket office and then to the castle. That building is one of the best fortified in the world, so we can talk more privately in there than out here."

If he wanted to avoid getting arrested again, I didn't know why we would go into a building filled with the Queen's armed soldiers, but I let him lead me inside. He bumped into a tiny Asian woman who was waiting in the ticket queue, typing rapidly on her smartphone.

"Sorry," he said in an English accent.

I gazed at him in amazement as he bought us two tickets to the castle. He handed the cashier two twenty-pound notes, and she handed him change. "Would you like to exchange your one-day pass for a year's pass? It's no extra charge and only available to UK residents."

"I'm all right today, thank you," Sam answered, still in a perfect accent.

"Keep your ticket, and if you change your mind you can get a stamp upon exit and change it then."

"Cheers," he said and walked towards the castle entry security check point.

"What are we doing?" I asked as we removed our jackets and lay them, the leftover coins, and the red phone on the security conveyor. I had nothing else to scan.

"Empty your pockets, sir," the security officer said to Sam.

"I'm all emptied out," he replied and held up his empty hands.

We walked through the scanner and picked up our meager belongings. Before I could put my jacket back on, Sam whispered, "Turn it inside out. We'll need to trade it out as soon as we can."

I knew he wanted to keep us hidden from Blythe, so I obliged, even though that meant the seams and tag showed. The black lining and our English accents would confuse anyone looking for an American woman in a red trench coat.

Sam walked quickly past the first gift shop and merged with a group of Americans.

I looked up at my husband. "Where's your wallet and phone?"

He slowed down his steps and lowered his voice so that I could barely hear him. "The police took them when Blythe had me arrested, but they didn't give them back when I left. They said they had no record that I entered with any possessions."

We followed the pavement alongside the tall gray stone walls. Short clipped green grass covered the lawn. A round tower loomed overhead. Along the way, uniformed soldiers with long rifles stood at impassive attention. Unlike the police, who could only hit me with a baton, I knew they could do more harm with their guns.

Two ladies wearing midi-length navy coats with brass buttons and perky navy caps above their hair buns stood at a crossroad. "Queen Mary's dollhouse and the State Rooms are to your left," they recited as they guided the visitors towards the left pathway.

I continued to speak to Sam under my breath. "What about your passport?" I asked.

"They took that, too. But I know it was Blythe who ended up with everything. She would want to analyze my phone and what's in my wallet. She should know me better than that, though." He paused for a moment. "The only bad thing is she'll keep both our passports to prevent us from leaving the country."

This sounded like a spy movie. Analyze my purse. Prevent us from the leaving the country. Maybe there was a secret room under the castle where Blythe and blonde Polish women were running computer analyses on our belongings and wiping us off the grid.

"Well, how did you buy our tickets to the castle without your wallet?" My list of questions was getting longer rather than shorter.

"I borrowed some money from an acquaintance."

I remembered the woman my careful husband had "bumped into" in the queue. He must have pickpocketed her. *What kind of person would do something like that?* Then I remembered the sketchy activities I had resorted to in the past two days.

Now the castle walls were on our right, and we could look over the protective outer wall that towered over the town of Windsor and Eton below. A group of school children played football and screamed in play below us. "Can't we go to the US Embassy and get their help? Surely they can get us passports and—"

Sam shook his head to silence me as we caught up with the crowd queuing up to enter the portion of Windsor Castle that displayed Queen Mary's dollhouse. I'd seen pictures of the elaborate six-foot-tall dollhouse online and knew it was housed and spotlighted in a big dark room. When I had planned our trip at home, Sam had said I could go see the dollhouse without him while he went to view the weapons in the State Rooms. Now he entered and firmly pulled my hand to follow him.

As we entered and showed our ticket stubs, a guide spoke pleasantly to us. "If you have any questions, please ask one of the docents in the rooms you are entering." I had questions all right, but none that a docent could answer for me.

A group of American ladies was chattering away. "Did you hear on your audio tour that everything in the dollhouse actually works? The toilets flush, the lights come on, and there's real wine in the wine barrels. This is awesome. I wish I could be a queen."

"Me, too," said her friend. "My guide said real authors wrote the miniature books and the words are really inside. This is so cool."

We followed the group into the display room and Sam leaned against a wall in the semi-dark. I whispered, "What about the embassy? Can't they help us?"

"They might help us, but they are in London, and in the meantime, Blythe is playing dirty and it could get worse. She's not going to let us get into London easily without a fight to get it back."

"Since we are in a spy movie, can we use a code word for whatever it is you have and won't give back so we don't have to keep saying that?" I wanted him to think I was on his side for now. I wasn't sure that I wasn't, but I was confused.

"How about 'Mary,'" he said, nodding to the dollhouse.

"Mary," I repeated. "That's too close to my name. How about Elizabeth?"

"Like the queen?"

I nodded. "Like the queen."

Tourist after tourist circled the dollhouse, took pictures on their phones, and moved to the next room. We seemed safely hidden for a while. "Keep talking," I said.

Sam continued to whisper answers to my questions. "I refused to give Elizabeth to Blythe for reasons I can explain in a minute. But what I was immediately worried about was that I left you in the pub with that woman and a gun." I nodded my head, remembering.

"No one was with me downstairs. I was alone and when I went back upstairs, I couldn't find you anywhere."

Sam nodded too. "I realized the waitress used the threat of you getting hurt to lure me into the car with Blythe. I told her that Elizabeth was in our hotel room. I figured that would buy me some time, and I could get help at the hotel and get back to rescue you, but Blythe is shrewd. She said she'd already been to my hotel room and knew Elizabeth wasn't there. In fact, she said, nothing was in my hotel room anymore."

"That's right," I said. "I went back to our room to see if you were there, and there wasn't even a record of us checking in. All our stuff was gone. I mean *everything*—clothes, shoes, luggage, toiletries, your reading glasses. The only thing in there was this." I handed him the red phone. "She keeps calling me on this and telling me what to do. She probably tracked me with it, too, but when I tried to get rid of it at the train station in Slough, it found me again at the train station in Windsor."

He glanced at me and chuckled. "You took the train to Slough and tried to get rid of the phone?"

I shrugged. "Well my idea didn't work. She scared me into keeping it after that."

He leaned closer and kissed my forehead. "You're always surprising me, Marion Martin."

He stared at the phone, turned it over, opened it, and handed it back to me. "Well, then, she probably knows we're in here by now, but she won't be able to track the phone in here. The walls of this fortress are too thick and there's a scrambling mechanism to thwart satellite tracking devices. The Crown spares no expense to protect itself, but its biggest asset here are thousand-year-old thick stone walls."

"You should be a tour guide," I whispered.

Sam took the phone from me and bent down. "I'm going to leave the phone here on the floor. Let's try to get out of here and blend in as much as possible with the tourists. It's easiest to get lost in a crowd, but there's only one way out of the castle, so we've got to be careful."

He tried to take my hand again, but I pulled it back and braced myself against the wall behind me. "I won't go with you until you tell me more about Elizabeth. Is she Blythe's? Is she illegal? Are you selling drugs or diamonds or what?"

He lowered his voice even more and spoke slowly. "Marion, please trust me. I will tell you everything, but right now we need to get out of here. I will take care of you, but we need to get to a more secure location."

My thoughts argued back that he wasn't very trustworthy, and he obviously couldn't take care of me seeing as how he had spent the night in jail and I had spent the night homeless. But I was more afraid of Blythe and her weird colleagues than I was of Sam for the moment. I let him take my hand, and we circled around the dollhouse to the exit and joined in with another group of loudly talking American tourists.

"I just love this palace! The queen comes here, you know, on the weekends. I wonder if Princess Charlotte is here today. Wouldn't that be awesome if her nanny was bringing her to see the dollhouse while we're here?"

"That would be awesome! I don't know if this is a palace, though. It's called Windsor Castle, and the other one in London is called Buckingham Palace," her friend said.

"What's the difference? We get to see Buckingham tomorrow. I'm so excited!"

"Let's ask the docent about the difference between a palace and castle."

One of the women turned to me. "Oh, I love your coat," she said in a lovely Southern accent. "It's inside out, you know, but I see the

Karl Lagerfeld tag. Is it from Paris? We wanted to go, but our trip isn't long enough."

Sam leaned over and muttered, "You've got to get rid of your coat."

It was time for my party-trick French. "Oh. Thees old thing. Oui, I mean, yes, I got it in Paree. Many years ago. It is, how do you say, veentage. It is rouge and warm for theez cold Engleesh weathur."

"Oh, are you French? Maybe I can find a vintage coat here. That would be so cool. I like name brands," said the woman. She was wearing a short tan jacket, straight out of L.L. Bean.

"There are many tres bon shops that you would like veery much in Paree," I said. "I don't know about a nice shop heere." I made a pouf sound of disdain and shrugged my shoulders. "Your coat is nice, too. It ees from Amereeca, oui? I ave an idee."

I shed the coat, turned it right side out, and held it up to her. "Thees rouge will look so nice with your blue eyes and air color. We could...how do you say...trade."

"Are you serious? It's from Paris? Amanda, what do you think? She said her jacket's from Paris and she'll trade me!"

The blonde smiled. "Sounds like a bargain to me. Didn't you get your jacket from Belk? A Paris jacket is way better than from the mall. If you don't want it, I'll trade her."

My brunette friend exclaimed and pulled her tan rain jacket off and handed it to me. "Deal!"

"Deal," I repeated. "Let me check dee pockets to make sure I deed not leave anything."

I pretended to check the pockets and handed her my red coat. She put it on, and I nodded with a smile. "Oui, eet looks very nice on you. Good-bye."

Sam grabbed my hand. "Au revoir," Sam said, as if it was natural, and waved good-bye to the women. I blinked in surprise. My husband did not speak French. In fact, he'd always said it was a sissy country with a sissy language.

From the corner where Sam had left the phone, I heard ringing. "She's calling me!" I said.

"Leave it," said Sam.

I pulled on my new tan coat, and we hurried towards the castle exit. From there, we retraced our steps to the crossroads and turned right towards St George's Chapel and another gift shop. There would be no time today to see where Henry the VIII was buried or where the Knights of the Garter had their special seats and banners bearing their coats of arms. "Maybe we should get our ticket stamped so we can come back again later this year," I said hopefully.

Sam shook his head in amazement. "Marion, we don't have any time for that. Blythe won't be able to find the phone signal and that will not improve her mood. When we get to the exit, she'll probably be waiting for us. If we see one of those women or the black cab, we're going to run in the opposite direction." He paused for a second. "The plan is to get to the train station. We need to get out of this town."

He joined the pace of the crowd we had overtaken, and we pushed in amongst them. As we exited the castle's iron gates, I put my head down like I'd noticed Sam doing. We kept as close as possible to the group of people who were walking towards the train station.

"Well done with the jacket bit," Sam said, hardly moving his mouth. "I'm impressed." If I hadn't been so scared, I would have loved bragging a little and speaking more French.

"Where are we taking the train?" I asked, imitating his low voice and trying not to move my mouth too much either. "I sent Freya a Facebook message telling her I lost my phone and purse while you were in…while you were gone. I was hoping she could lend me some money or even come get me." I remembered that I hadn't had a way to see if she'd responded.

Sam glanced at me and barely smiled. "I'm impressed again. I agree we should head to Freya's. That's in Bath, right? If Blythe has someone watching us, they will most likely think we are going to London. We could take a train to Reading instead and then go to Bath to meet with Freya. That should throw Blythe off our trail for now."

There were so many unanswered questions. I thought it would be easier to talk on the train, and now that we didn't have the red phone, maybe Blythe wouldn't find us. We walked slowly through the train station. It was bustling with shoppers and tourists snapping selfies on their smartphones. "Be ready to pop into a shop or café at any sign of one of the three women," Sam muttered.

Sam spotted the hotel clerk who had checked us in and turned out to be Blythe's driver. She was standing in front of a restaurant called Bill's and had full view of the only entrance to the train. "There's blondie number one. We need a plan B."

"We could take a boat to Bath instead of the train. I saw lots of boats on the Thames this morning." I hoped I was being helpful and not stupid.

"Good plan B. Let's cut down this side passage and head towards the river. Keep your head down and don't look back."

I wrapped my new tan coat tightly around me and hoped I looked different. We held hands and walked quickly away from the station, down a side mews with adorable shop fronts, and towards the river. Finally, the Thames came into view.

Sam went into a miniature house that rented boats and sold tickets for tours, canoes, and dinner cruises. After a few minutes, he returned and shook a boat key at me. I followed him to a small dock where a white speed boat with a nice brown wood-like interior was locked up.

"Where did you get the money this time?" I asked.

"I had to use my credit card. We'll have to hurry, because Blythe will be able to track us in a few minutes. In fact, we'll have to ditch the boat as soon as we can, so be thinking of a plan C."

I thought we were probably on plan D by now, but I got the point that we were trackable. "I didn't think you had your wallet," I said.

"I learned to hide a card or cash in my shoe. I also have a hundred-dollar bill, but that won't help us here. And I have a credit card, but I didn't want to use it unless it was absolutely necessary."

While he explained, Sam untied the boat and helped me climb in. "How can *she* track your credit card?" I asked. "I thought only the credit card company could do that."

"You saw what she did earlier with a mobile phone. I think she hacked the police department's computer system to show herself as a high ranking official, which made her able to have me arrested. She couldn't keep me past the time I was released, though, without formal charges and without letting me have a court-appointed solicitor."

As Sam confidently steered us away from the dock and his short dark brown hair ruffled in the breeze, I briefly reminisced about boating with the boys on the lake in the summer. We always had a lot of fun when the boys were younger, but when Sam started working overseas more frequently, we all complained that we missed our captain. Instead of staying home more, he chose to teach Wills and Bear how to drive our boat. They really enjoyed the responsibility and how it made them feel older, but I was annoyed. I pushed the memory away because I had to help think of what to do next.

We boated through the town centre at the maximum speed to avoid the queen's swans. I wanted Sam to floor it and take us all the way to the Atlantic Ocean and home to Ohio.

I yelled to Sam over the motor. "She told me you have to give her Elizabeth in twenty-four hours, or we won't make it. Does that mean she'll put us both in jail? Why can't you give whatever it is back to her or at least turn it in to the police?"

"Blythe is not planning to arrest us, Marion. She's planning worse. Elizabeth doesn't belong to her or to the police or to me. I need to get it to my boss. Blythe used to work *with* me, but now she works *against* me. She just used the police to try to intimidate me and you into giving her back what she wants. She was showing off that she can infiltrate the pub, the hotel, the police, and even the British government at Windsor Castle by tracking us there. She'll be able to find us from the credit card I just used. She does have some power, but her new boss is not one of the good guys. We need to get to a safe place for me to be able to contact my director and get Elizabeth to a safe place or into the right hands."

Sam scanned the shores, which were lined with brownish-red-brick historical buildings. Previously homes for the wealthy, they had been turned into restaurants and apartments. Walking paths meandered along the river. I was glad that England had preserved its history. We examined each boat we encountered to determine if it was a dinner cruiser, a speed boat like the one we were in, or my favourite, a houseboat. So far, there was no sign of Blythe.

Once we left the lovely town of Windsor, the river wound amongst beautiful green pastures with fluffy white sheep grazing. What appeared to be a grand home was set back behind weeping willow trees. What a treat this would have—or should have—been.

I turned to Sam. "What is it? What do you have that's so

valuable? And *where* is it? You said it's not drugs." I beseeched him to help me believe that he wasn't really a bad guy and I wasn't some blind mafia wife.

He glanced at me and then back to the front of the boat. "Marion, I love you very much and I really did want to have a do-over on this trip. Anything I've ever hidden from you has truly been for your and the boys' protection. I am not doing anything illegal, and I haven't done anything illegal." Well, I thought, he *had* picked someone's pocket, but I chose not to mention it right then, and he continued. "But what my job has entailed over all the years is highly secretive—for my clients' protection and my family's. Mar, I work for the good guys, but sometimes we get tempted to do bad things because we see it and are around it.

"Blythe got tempted on our last assignment together. Our Elizabeth is very powerful, and that's what Blythe wants back. I know it may be hard, but I really need you to trust me, to believe that I want to get this taken care of without either of us getting hurt. Whenever I don't tell you something, like what or where, it's for your protection. If you don't know anything, then you're worthless to Blythe and she'll only be after me. She may use you to try to get to me, but she knows that as long as you're alive, I might help her. But if something happens to you, all bets are off."

I wanted to ask what he'd been tempted by, but I was too scared once again to learn the answer. "Does this mean that you aren't in computer sales?"

"I'll explain everything as I get a chance. In the meantime, I just need you to trust me."

Once we left Windsor, we met fewer boats. When we were the only ones we could see, Sam steered the boat over to a bank with some small trees. After securing the boat to one of the trees, he stepped out and held his hand out to me. "Are you ready for a walk in the English countryside? I thought this was what you always wanted to do."

His smile seemed genuine and he *had* held his hand to help me out like a perfect gentleman, but I hesitated. *Was this true?* All we had to do was get to someplace where he could contact his director and hand over the mysterious Elizabeth. I could handle that, I guessed.

I gracefully took his hand like a lady and climbed out of the boat. Once I was on the bank, Sam untied the line and shoved the boat away from the bank. We stood and watched as it floated away on the current.

We climbed up the bank to a public footpath. A delightful black wooden sign shaped like an arrow read "MAIDENHEAD 2 MILES."

I took my husband's hand, and we began our country walk. It wasn't exactly how I had imagined it, but for the moment it felt right.

4

Boats, Bikes, and Bath

In the distance, we heard the sound of a motorboat, and Sam pulled me along the path away from the river. If the boat was Blythe and her cronies, they'd see our boat and know exactly where we had gotten out.

"Our country walk is over," said Sam. "It's time for a country run!"

As we sprinted up the path, I panted, "Shouldn't we get off the path and hide?" We were surrounded on both sides by meadows of wildflowers. We could lie down in the flowers but that seemed useless. My thoughts drifted to the graveyard where Wills is buried. Every week for the past year, I had taken a bouquet of wildflowers and stayed for an hour or so to tell him what we'd been doing that week, pray, and tell him that we missed him. Mom had agreed to go for me while Sam and I were in Europe.

I spotted two barns and a wooden enclosure filled with fluffy white sheep and pointed. Sam nodded, and we turned and ran for the fence.

The sounds we heard stopped. Since they hadn't gradually faded away, I guessed the motorboat had stopped near where we'd left ours.

Once they saw the boat was empty, they would easily surmise we had left the river.

My normal physical activities involved sitting in the bleachers watching Bear play soccer and driving him around, so by this time, I felt a piercing pain in my side. Spurred on by fear and by Sam's urging me to keep going, I followed him in a clumsy climb over the fence into the pen of sheep.

They were not as white up close, but they were still cute, and thankfully seemed oblivious to the two strange humans who had joined them. The only problem was that they'd eaten the grass down to the ground and we were exposed.

I instinctively got down low. We crawled, using the sheep as buffers as we worked our way toward one of the barns. We looked around for a farmer or worker, but saw no one. "Let's get inside the barn and find a place to hide," Sam whispered.

It was darker inside. As our eyes adjusted, I could see a couple of ewes and some chickens in pens.

Sam gestured towards several bales of hay. He entered the enclosure and hid behind them while I peeked out a window facing the direction we'd come from. Three female figures emerged from the tall grasses.

"They're following us," I whispered. "Will they think we stayed on the footpath? They won't come this way, will they?"

I hadn't thought to be more careful not to leave a trail to follow and I was ashamed. I had been a den mother for William and Bear's scout troop, and we had learned all about things like this.

A fat sheep in the pen next to us pushed against the fencing to reach the bales. "Greedy sheep," I said. "Eat your own hay."

Sam glanced at me and laughed. "You look cute with straw in your hair."

"Stop flirting with me! This is an emergency!" I threw a wad of straw at him, but it gently floated in the air and missed him entirely. The sheep turned to look at us but kept chewing.

"What do we do?" I asked.

Sam thought for a moment. "We had our country walk. Are you ready for a bike ride through the countryside?"

"Bike ride?"

"Yes. I saw some bikes leaning against the other barn."

"When did you see those?" I said.

"You looked out the window twice, Marion. Didn't you see them?"

"Well, no, but I was looking for Blythe and the farmer."

"It's my job to look around and pay attention to my surroundings. I really messed up with that at the Two Brewers. You distracted me," Sam said. I was about to get upset but then I realized he meant distracting in a positive way.

I couldn't believe we were chitchatting away as if we were sipping wine in a cozy pub rather than hiding in a barn, but I decided to follow Sam's relaxed lead. He leaned closer. "Blythe will probably do what we did—go through the sheep pen, then come in here. We need to find a different way out and circle back around to the other barn and borrow those bikes."

"Borrow?" I said. I had to admit borrowing *did* feel better than stealing.

"We can walk along the back wall and see if there's another door. If there's not, we can climb out one of the windows."

One ewe baahed as we edged past her. I was sure the sound was loud enough to attract attention. "We're not here to hurt you. We're here to help you," I whispered, hoping to calm her down with a quote from *Lord of the Rings*.

61

Our inspection revealed that there wasn't another door. "We'll have to climb out a window," Sam whispered. He peeked out the closest window. "They've reached the pen. We have to hurry. They'll be at the barn soon." He sounded calm, but my insides were twisted in knots.

The sheep outside started baaing again, a signal that the women were getting close. I hurried behind Sam to a window on a different wall of the barn. He clasped his hands together low enough for me to step on and I put one foot in his hands and braced my other foot on his thigh. Normally I would have been self-conscious of my weight, but I didn't care at all this time. I got one leg over the window, and half-fell, half-parkoured onto the ground below.

Sam climbed through the window. "Go grab a bike," he said.

I nodded, followed the edge of the barn to the corner, and ran to the bikes, grabbing the first one that seemed my size. When I pulled it away from the tangle of others, they all fell over with a crash. "So much for stealth," said Sam.

"There they are," I yelped, and Sam turned back to where I was looking. I could see only two women, neither of whom was Blythe, so I assumed she was inside the barn.

We pedaled as hard as we could on a path that ran between a farmhouse and another field on its way to the main road. I felt like eyes were on me and was sure that a farmer was going to come running out of the house shouting, "Stop, thief!" and shooting at us.

Sam seemed to sense what I was thinking, because he muttered, "Don't worry, the kids are probably at school and farmers don't usually have guns."

I breathed a momentary sigh of relief. *That's right*, I thought, *people don't carry guns in England. But then again, bad girls do and probably farmers who hunt do too.*

I decided not to be contrary and to follow Sam as fast as I could down the driveway and onto the road. He seemed to know intuitively which direction to go. We stayed on the pavement, because the road seemed too narrow to fit two lanes of cars and bikes.

On one side of the road, blackberry briars trailed over our path and the thorns snagged my new jacket. On the right side, cars flew past us. I flinched every time—still thinking we were on the wrong side of the road.

We'd ridden a few miles when we saw signs for Slough. "My goal for now is to get us on a train," Sam said as we paused at an intersection. "Keep your eyes out, especially for black cabs."

"Great," I muttered. *Would this day never end?* My thighs were now burning, but I kept pumping the pedals and following Sam, who was cautiously following the road into town. When we reached the town limits, Sam turned down a side street.

After whimsical Windsor, Slough was quite industrial looking. Shops with busy and tasteless signs ran down the street, while red-bricked apartments sat on top. We couldn't ride on the pavement any longer as it was packed with pedestrians walking hurriedly by, most holding orange plastic shopping bags. Sam gracefully slid off his bike and parked it on a rack. I awkwardly got off beside him and slid my bike next to his.

"Should we lock them up?" I asked, instantly realizing that it was ridiculous for me to consider locking up bikes we'd stolen from some unsuspecting farmer. When Sam rolled his eyes, I said, "Never mind," although I still felt guilty over what we'd done.

Sam scanned the street. "Let's find the train station," he said, "but be ready to duck into a shop if a black cab passes by." He turned and walked confidently to the right. *How did he know which way to go? I was the one who'd actually been in the Slough train station, and*

Blythe must have come there, too, since the phone I'd left on the platform had found its way back to me.

We passed a supermarket called Sainbury's. Everyone who came through the doors was carrying an orange bag, so that mystery was solved. The thought of food sounded really good—my baguette was long used up. My mind drifted. Maybe I would lose a few pounds on this trip. That would be a plus.

I saw a street sign pointing the way to the train station. It said it was a six-minute walk. *How could it claim that? What if I walked faster or slower than the average person?*

Sam stopped on the corner. "Blythe will probably think we're heading to London. I'll have to double-check the train times, but I think there's a train to Reading every twenty minutes or so. Hopefully we can get on the next one before they get here."

About that time, it began to sprinkle, and practically everyone walking pulled out an umbrella. One has to be prepared for rain every day in England, I supposed. I discovered that my new raincoat had a hood zipped into the collar and I pulled it over my hair. I couldn't have looked any worse than I already did, but I tried to preserve my dignity as much as possible.

We reached the station, which, from the outside—a view I hadn't experienced—was charming. It was made of the same red brick as the buildings in town, but the roof was rounded in a pleasing manner and covered in gables and chimney pots. We walked inside, and I kept my hood on.

Sam gestured toward a line of ticket machines. "You stay here and keep an eye out. Say 'sheep' if you see anyone. I'll get our tickets."

I kept my eyes peeled for three blonde women. It was rush hour, and people were either hurrying to the platforms or standing together all looking up at a screen displaying the train times. An announcer spoke with a pleasing British accent, "The next train to London Paddington is stopping at Platform Three. Thank you for using Great Western Railway."

As the message ended, the crowd of onlookers moved as one group toward Platform Three. I saw a woman with a blonde ponytail, and my heart skipped a beat. Before I could say, "Sheep!" the woman turned slightly, and I could see she wasn't one of the three pursuing us. A new group gathered under the departure screen and I felt Sam touch my elbow.

"I have tickets for the next train on Platform Two for Reading. From there, if all goes well, we'll take a train to Bath and find Freya."

I nodded and followed him to the platform. We put our tickets in the turnstile and walked through. "How did you buy the tickets?" I asked in a low voice. "You said if you use your credit card, she'll know where we are and where we're going."

"Exactly. I withdrew some pounds from the bank machine and bought two tickets to Reading with the cash, then used my credit card to buy two tickets to London. She may be able to see I withdrew money, but she won't know what I bought with it. Hopefully the tickets to London will throw her off for a bit," Sam said.

I felt exposed on the platform as we waited for the train. *What if Blythe came through the turnstile or what if she was on the train coming to Slough and got off on our platform?* We were trapped with nowhere to hide.

"Here," Sam said, thrusting a copy of the *Evening Standard* into my hands. "Follow me." He held his own copy of the newspaper open and appeared to be reading it as he walked. He found an empty spot on a wall and stood with his back to it next to a small group of people also waiting for the train. I imitated his actions and felt safer blending in with the crowd.

A whistle blew, and two railroad men in black uniforms told us all to stand away from the platform. The train roared in and came to a squealing halt in front of us. Passengers poured off, and as soon as the departing passengers disembarked, we joined the group getting on.

The train car was packed with people. "Let's stand back here," Sam said, and led me to a spot near an area where luggage was stacked. "Hold on to this bar and keep your paper up. Reading's not far from here."

I braced myself by holding onto the bar with one hand and used the other hand to hold the paper. It was a black and white blur, but I did read some headlines: *TORY MP BANNED. SYRIAN REFUGEE FOUND DEAD. SPICE GIRLS REUNION TOUR.* Would tomorrow's headline be *AMERICAN COUPLE THROWN FROM TRAIN?*

The train stopped at the next station and some seats were freed up. Sam pushed me gently towards two and we sat down.

For the first time in hours, I felt like I could breathe. Sam reached over and pushed a strand of hair behind my ear. It tickled a little, but I didn't care because I loved the way he was looking down at me. His stomach rumbled in hunger and mine responded with a growl. Although I was sure that I looked a mess, I leaned my head on his shoulder.

He opened his copy of the *Standard* over both of us. I must have dozed off, because when the train stopped with a whistle and we heard "Reading" on the loudspeaker, I jerked awake and jumped to my feet. "It's all right," Sam said gently. "We're here. You only slept a few minutes, but you needed it. It's been quite the day so far."

We walked with the crowd up an escalator and crossed one landing to reach another. As busy and crowded as the station was, everyone was polite and calm. On the right side of the escalators, people stood in a straight line so passengers on the left side could pass. It was just like on the roads.

Everything was orderly and quiet for such a large crowd. No loud American voices here, only men and women in suits bearing briefcases and laptop bags and their exit tickets. Occasionally, a person in a suit would break into a run to catch a train, but even that seemed civilized.

"Do we get on a train to Bath now?" I asked.

Sam shook his head. "I didn't buy tickets to Bath in Slough. We'll exit here, and you can be look-out again while I get them here. I still have cash."

We put our tickets back through the turnstile and walked through. It was raining hard now but we didn't have to go outside. Sam went to the ticket kiosks, and I stood with my back to him and looked around. "These aren't working," he grumbled. "I'll have to get in the queue and buy the tickets at the sales counter."

"Remember to say, "Bath" as in "cloth" so you don't sound American," I whispered to him.

Freya had taught me that trick about Bath. She said you can always tell the tourists by how they pronounce English towns. That's how I knew Reading sounded like the color red. Slough had stumped me, though. I punched Sam. "Should I stay in the line with you? Or can you give me some money? I'll get us some food while you get the tickets."

"Food sounds great," said Sam. "They did feed me in jail. It wasn't the best food, but it was edible. What did you do? Have you had anything to eat since our fish and chips?" he said.

"Oh, yes," I said sarcastically. "I had a delicious baguette with butter and strawberry jam and the best cup of coffee ever."

"How did you get that without any money?"

"I'll tell you all about my exciting twenty-four hours without you when we have time later," I said and held my hand out for money.

"I can't wait. You've been amazing about all this." He handed me two oversized bills with Queen Elizabeth's face. "Here are two tenners. Still be careful walking around, but I think we're okay for now. Meet me back at the turnstile when you're done."

I nodded, took the money, and walked to a group of small shops and cafes. They reminded me of a miniature food court at an American mall. I stopped at a kiosk selling sandwiches and crisps and used my best Australian accent, wondering if I should buy two beers to be more authentic. We needed caffeine, though, so I got two coffees instead.

I could see Sam was still buying tickets, and I really needed to use the loo. I kept looking from side to side, but no one seemed familiar. I passed more fast food restaurants and small shops. I was surprised to see a Burger King, but everything else was new to me.

I dodged into the WC, and as soon as I went inside, I wanted to kick myself for not telling Sam where I was going. This was, after all, how I lost him the last time.

I hurriedly finished and went back to the main area of the station as fast as possible. Sam wasn't at the ticket counter or anywhere else. I walked, scanning the shops and eateries while my heart pounded like a jackhammer. *You idiot,* I thought. I reached the turnstiles, but he wasn't there.

Then I heard a voice. "Keep your head down as much as possible as we go through the station, and whenever you see a camera, turn away from it. Try to be unobtrusive and keep changing up your accent if you have to talk."

I turned to see my husband, now wearing a pair of sunglasses and a hat. "Accessorize!" he said and nodded to a store with the same name. I smiled in relief and obediently put my head down as we walked through the turnstiles to board our train to Bath. I was secretly pleased. Freya aside, Bath had been one of my must-sees in England—Jane Austen had once lived there.

The train wasn't as crowded as the one to Reading had been, so we quickly found seats together. It was getting dark, and I couldn't see out the window, but the drops sliding down told me it was still raining. After the accident, I had avoided driving in the rain, but for some reason, on the train it was comforting.

We pulled trays out from the seats in front of us and tucked into our bacon and cheese sammies with salt and vinegar crisps. The coffee didn't taste as good as the cup I'd bought earlier in the day, but I was grateful for the warmth, the calories, and the caffeine.

The ride to Bath would take about an hour, and I was hopeful that we had given Blythe the slip. I took advantage of the time to ask Sam a bunch of questions, and to his credit, he patiently answered.

"So the time you didn't show up to Wills' tenth birthday party when we'd rented out the skating rink for his whole class and the neighborhood kids and you said that your boss said you had to stay in Rome to close the sale or not show back up at work…is that what really happened?"

Sam shifted uncomfortably in his seat.

"No, that's not what really happened. We had a client from an Arabic country who needed our protection. He was meeting with an opposing political party to try to bring economic help to his country. The operation went wrong, and we had to get him to a safe place and stay with him until we were certain that all was well.

"I really wanted to be at Wills' birthday, Mar, and I felt awful that we planned the whole skate party and I got his hopes up. Then, it seemed to everyone that I was a workaholic and a bad dad."

"Well, you still *do* seem like a workaholic, Sam," I said. "Isn't this mess we're in right now because of your job?"

"Well, sorta. But I think of a workaholic as someone who gets financial or ego-boosting dividends. I think of my job as helping people who need my specific skillset to keep the world a better and safer place. I'm talking about countries that may be at war and economies that may be failing, but my role helps keep people in the U.S. happily supplying birthday parties to innocent children—even if they're not my own."

He paused for a moment. "Blythe was one of the good guys for a long time, but I guess just like in all the cop movies, someone's partner gets tempted by the bad side and joins their team. Trust me, Mar, Elizabeth would ruin many families' birthday parties." He smiled down at me. "My new partner," he said, as he placed his hand over mine, "will help win one for the good side. Does this make sense?"

"It makes sense. But it really sounds like a movie. I just hate thinking about all the times I believed what you told me, only to find now that they weren't real."

"What's real is that I love you and our family, even your mother. I really believed that keeping my work undercover was protecting all who are important to me. Now I need your help to keep protecting our family and friends—and perhaps some complete strangers."

"OK," I said. "I understand, and I do want to help." I still had worries and questions spilling through my mind, but I decided to quash them and become, at least for now, Sam's new partner against crime. "Does this mean you work for our government, like the military or FBI?"

"Not exactly," he said. "After we drop Elizabeth off to the right people, I will explain more. Can you wait until then?"

"I guess so," I said. "I've waited this long."

Sam squeezed my hand. "Now, tell me about what happened to you while I was in jail. No one would tell me where you were. I was scared for you and praying so hard."

"That's what I did, too. I prayed a lot."

I thought back over the day. "Actually, I slept in a church and lots of people helped me. An old man with a dog walked me to the police station but it was closed. Some people gave me enough money to buy breakfast. And a teenage girl let me use her phone. That's how I sent a message to Freya on Facebook."

He kissed my forehead. "You'll have to tell me all about it. I'm impressed, but not surprised."

A lovely British voice announced that we were arriving at Bath. I felt relieved to know that soon we'd see Freya and have a shower, a bed, and some food. "Maybe Freya has some clothes I can borrow," I said. "After all, we used to share everything."

Sam nodded and glanced around the station, ignoring me for the most part. "Remember to keep your head down and stay with the crowds. We want to blend in so we're hard to pick out."

I dutifully squeezed in between the passengers disembarking from the train. I inched in much closer to the group in front of me than I'd been taught was polite, but I didn't really care about being polite just then. I kept my face down and, as we approached the exit turnstiles, Sam took my hand and almost dragged me out of the Bath Station and onto the street.

He walked purposefully and I lengthened my stride to keep up with him, all the while wondering if he'd ever been here before for one of his "missions." I used that word in my mind to make the past lies more bearable.

It was hard to keep my head down because I wanted to look everywhere. It was already dark, but I could see that Bath was lovely.

Its lighting showed off creamy-colored limestone buildings and I could see the steeple of a stately cathedral not far away.

Sam steered us away from the church and up a steep side street, and I tried to keep my eyes down on the cobblestone walk. An arched bridge crossed the river, and it was lit up, too. I couldn't help thinking that it was prettier than the Christmas lights in my hometown.

Plenty of people were walking around—romantic couples, families. A tour group was stopped in front of a gorgeous building where a distinguished-looking top-hatted gentleman on a stool talked to them. I could hardly contain myself when what looked like a parade of Regency-dressed gentlemen and ladies walked down the hill in our direction. They looked like extras in a Jane Austen movie, and I stopped, ready to take pictures of them.

"What are you doing?" muttered Sam. "We have to keep going."

Then I remembered that I didn't have my phone. I would have to take a picture in my mind just like a lady from the seventeen-hundreds would have done. Then, like the good spy I was becoming, I turned my face away from the delightful scene and quickened my pace to keep up with Sam.

He turned down a lovely street that had shops on the ground floor and apartments above. Every building was the same cream-colored stone and was decorated with flower-filled window boxes or hanging baskets. The shops all had charming window displays like something out of an old black-and-white Christmas movie, and I hoped there would be time for me to browse them in daylight after we got rid of Elizabeth.

Sam stopped by one of the doors and pushed the buzzer. "Freya lives here," he muttered.

It was obvious now that he'd been here before. When I'd asked him if we could visit Bath and Freya when I was planning the trip, he'd given me the impression that he barely remembered my college roommate. Another lie. That meant Freya was a liar, too.

A speaker crackled and I heard a familiar English voice. "Hello?" Sam spoke in a low voice. "It's me, Sam…and Marion."

"I wasn't expecting you so soon but come on up." The door clicked open with a buzz.

I could see now that Freya lived in one of the apartments above an antique bookshop. Through the shop window, I could see a delightful area with antique leather chairs and side tables with lamps for sitting and reading. Obviously, the owner wanted the patrons to sit and stay for a while, but because of these two liars, I couldn't enjoy it. Neither could I enjoy the narrow dark staircase we walked up, lit with old golden candelabras that showed the emerald carpet and matching striped wallpaper.

Given what I'd just learned, I was nervous about how I was supposed to act around Freya. I decided to follow Sam's lead and try not to talk too much. About that time, Sam leaned back towards me and said, "Follow my lead and try not to talk too much." I opened my mouth to say something and then shut my mouth and squeezed my lips together. This was going to be harder than I thought.

I heard my old roommate's voice from up above us. "Don't worry, just one more flight to go. I've put the kettle on." She held the door open for us, and when we walked in, she squeezed me and kissed each cheek. "It's been too long," she said in her lovely English accent, the one that began my quest of acquiring a perfect accent myself. "I can't believe it took you over twenty years to finally come visit me."

It didn't take Sam *twenty years to finally come visit you*, I thought, but I just kissed her back like the nice person I am.

"You look just the same," I said and meant it. Her ginger hair had a few grey strands and her creamy face had a line or two, but her light blue eyes and sweet smile were just the same. My resolve crumpled. Maybe there was a perfectly reasonable explanation Sam knew how to get here. It would just be one more on an increasingly long list of unanswered questions.

Freya smiled at me as we followed her into a sitting room straight out of a Jane Austen movie. "Marion, you're the one who hasn't changed at all. You are just as lovely as ever."

I shook my head. "I'm a wreck," I said. "After losing our luggage I haven't been able to shower or change or anything. Did you get my Facebook message?"

"Yes, and I answered you," she said, surprised. "I thought you saw it and that was why you were here. I told you I could wire you some money if you still needed it, but you didn't answer."

My heart jumped, and I looked at Sam, but he laughed and calmly explained that our trip so far had been a series of mishaps. First, the airline had lost our luggage, he said, and then I left my purse which had his wallet, our passports, and mobiles on the back of a chair at a pub, which had subsequently been stolen. I blushed a little because I looked completely irresponsible in Sam's story, but Freya was all sympathy and concern.

"That's a rotten way to start your trip. I hope you won't judge England by one pickpocket," she said.

Sam continued. "Of course, I filed a claim with the police and the embassy, and they will get all this straightened out in the next few days. In the meantime, Marion thought we could rely upon your hospitality for a short time since we can't even check into a hotel these days without a passport." I blushed even more. According to Sam's version of events, it was all because of my blunder. Maybe next time I could be in charge of the cover story. At the same time, I was impressed with how quickly he came up with a perfectly reasonable explanation.

"You had enough money for the train tickets?" Freya asked.

"Yes," said Sam, "I had withdrawn some pounds from a bank machine before all this happened."

"That's a relief. Wouldn't want you to have to sing for your supper. I don't remember your singing voice being that great."

Sam laughed.

I was tired of the charade and getting hungrier and more irritated by the minute. "This is so pretty," I said, waving my hand around the room. I spun around to look at everything at once. Mr. Darcy would have felt at home on the grey velvet sofas and at the writing desk. Her intricate furniture and even the pictures on the wall would make any Austen lover quite happy.

"Arthur and I decked it out in proper Regency style so we can let it out to tourists who come for the Baths and Balls. I even have fancy dress for them to wear. We escape to his parents' home in Yorkshire."

"They wear fancy dresses to the Baths?" asked Sam, looking rough and out of place with his days-old stubble and wrinkled clothes.

Freya laughed and said, "No, to the *Balls* not the Baths. Everyone wears Regency fancy dress. Oh, what do you call it in the States? *Costumes*, yes, that's it. The ladies wear the long dresses, hats, and gloves, and the men wear top hats, riding trousers, and fluffy high-collared shirts. It's all the fashion several times a year, and we call the clothes 'fancy dress.'"

I looked at Sam. "Didn't you see the people all dressed up when we were walking here?"

He nodded. "Yes, I saw that, but it looked more silly than fancy to me."

Freya explained that her husband Arthur was away in London for business but that we would be able to meet her two children later when they got home from sporting events. "In fact, Tilly and James will be home any time now. Another mum is dropping them off."

Freya reassured us we could stay as long as necessary and she'd lend us anything we needed until we got our luggage back again. I let out a sigh of relief, and her kindness made my eyes well up with tears. I figured I would lose it soon if I didn't get some sleep and food.

My silent wish was granted. Freya led us upstairs to our bedroom with an en-suite and said she'd meet us in the kitchen whenever we were refreshed. "The wardrobe is stocked with Regency clothes if you are inclined to dress for dinner," she said, "but I'll grab some of Arthur's and my clothes and leave them outside your door if you want to dress like the downstairs."

I knew she was joking about servants and the upper class, but I could hardly smile by this point. Sam did better than me. He chuckled at her joke, thanked her, and shut the door.

I fell onto the creaking double bed draped in pink and green and fell asleep. Even though I was mad at her, I still felt safer in Freya's house than anywhere else I'd been the last two days. Sam must have felt so, too. I briefly heard him snore, but it didn't keep me awake.

We slept a couple of hours. When I woke, I took a reviving shower. It took me awhile to figure out that the light switch was on the bedroom wall rather than in the loo and that I had to flush by pulling down on a chain hanging from the ceiling, but other than that I enjoyed the modern shower, thankful it wasn't Regency era.

Sam brought in the clothes Freya left for us in the hallway and their sweaters and trousers fit us well. I had evidently lost the five pounds that I could never get to budge. Easy diet—don't eat dinner, snacks, or lunch, and have a baguette and coffee for breakfast. Get hardly any sleep and keep on the move all day and night. Basically, don't eat and you will lose weight. I just needed a better marketing approach than "Order the Homeless Diet Plan off Amazon today."

Once dressed, Sam and I went downstairs to find Freya. We'd slept so long that her children were already in their pajamas and enjoying a late-night cup of hot cocoa and biscuits at the kitchen table with their mum. Tilly and James jumped up politely when they saw us and came to shake our hands.

"Mummy said we could stay up late to see you, but we got worried you would sleep all night and we'd miss you," Tilly said in an adorable little singsong voice.

"We've been waiting ages to meet you," said James. "I want to learn about American football and Mummy said you were the people to ask."

Freya grinned at her children. "We'll badger them tomorrow about American football. Let me feed our guests while they rest at the table." She turned to Sam and me. "I have sausage and mash all ready and keeping warm in the cooker. Does that sound all right?"

"Sounds amazing," I said, and meant it.

Tilly cocked her head and looked at me with a quizzical expression. "Mummy has a jumper just like yours," she said.

I looked around for what she meant by jumper and realized she was referring to my sweater. "This *is* hers," I said. "Our airplane lost our luggage, so your mummy is letting me borrow it." I wondered if it was too late to get Bear to call me Mummy.

Sam and I sat down at the table and Freya made us plates of sausages and mashed potatoes slathered in gravy, each with a scoop of bright green peas on the side. I finally relaxed and enjoyed the home-cooked meal and the children's chatter about school, sports, and pushing for a dog.

Freya opened a bottle of red wine and poured the three adults a glass. I felt normal again in the cozy kitchen that, unlike the formal décor of the rest of the house, looked like a happy family lived there. School books were scattered around, crumbs were on the counter, and family pictures were posted on the refrigerator.

The children were younger than Bear—elementary age—but they made me miss him terribly. He was probably going to his orientation by now.

I leaned forward, soaking in their youthfulness and jokes and felt as if we were back to our planned holiday and not on a world threat mission. I could see stars and part of the moon peeking through the kitchen window and was relieved we had made it un-eventfully through the first half of the twenty-four hours. Tomorrow, we would hand off Elizabeth and hopefully be finally done with whatever she was.

Freya sipped from her glass of wine. "After I do the school run in the morning, would you like me to show you around Bath? The Roman Baths and Cathedral would be brilliant for you to see, and there is a Jane Austen festival with lots to participate in for that—dances, fancy dress, and historical exhibitions."

I froze with my wine glass raised halfway to my lips, wondering what Sam was going to say, but he responded casually. "Freya, thank you very much, but if you don't mind, I think we'll head back to bed soon and have a lie in tomorrow morning. We'll probably be ready in the afternoon to do some tourist bits."

"Absolutely, take your time. I have some work I can do in my shop downstairs. Did you see it when you walked by?"

"That beautiful bookstore?" I asked.

Tilly giggled. "No, that's not Mummy's shop. That belongs to Mr. Clarke. He doesn't like children to come into his dusty old store."

"Tilly, we've talked about that," scolded her mother.

"Sorry." Tilly pouted but perked up again. "Mummy's shop is on the other side of our apartment door. It's the apothecary store. Just like a real chemist's shop from historical times," she said proudly. "Mummy lets children come in and keeps a bowl of candy for them to have for free. All my friends like to go in there to get some, and we wave it at Mr. Clarke when we walk by his old store."

At that, the quieter James spoke up. "It's really funny to see his face when we walk by waving our candy at him. He hates candy because it might get his stupid old books sticky."

Freya looked at her children and feigned a frown. "You're giving a bad impression to our guests. I think that is the signal that it is time for you to go to bed."

The children hugged their mother and obediently left the room after telling us goodnight. Minutes later, I could hear giggling and doors shutting in another part of the house.

Freya made a face. "Ignore them, please. I've obviously complained about him in hearing of the kids too much. He *is* a grumpy old man, though."

She stood and pushed her chair under the table. "All right, I'll wash up, and no, you can't help. Sleep as late as you need to and make yourselves at home. Help yourself to tea and toast in the kitchen. Or would you want coffee? I can pick some up on the way back from the school run."

"Tea is great. When in England…" I responded with a giggle.

We said our goodnights to Freya and went back upstairs to our room. "Are we really going back to sleep now?" I asked Sam. "I thought it would be fun to have a catch-up chat with Freya."

"And risk saying something about Blythe or what's happening with us right now? I think it's better for you not to talk much. In fact, I wish you hadn't said it was okay to have the tea. If you hadn't spoken so quickly, I would have asked Freya, politely, of course, to bring us back some coffee. I need to buy us more alone time to use her computer and phone to try to make some contacts that will help us get Elizabeth to a safe zone." Sam's response was not exactly impatient, but his tone was like he was trying to explain something complicated to a child.

I felt resentful, because I was obviously not used to being a secret agent or spy or whatever we were doing, but he *had* told me to let him talk. I just didn't realize he meant about everything.

I offered to make up for my lack of earlier insight. "I can go back out to Freya and act like I didn't want to embarrass you but that you would rather have coffee," I said. "In fact, I could ask her if you can use her computer right now. I'm sure she wouldn't mind."

Sam shook his head. "Thanks, but that's okay. It's a good idea for us to get as much sleep as we can right now because I'm not sure what's going to happen tomorrow. I should have enough time to make contact while she's gone to take the kids to school."

He hopped onto the double bed, which seemed very small compared to our king-sized bed at home, and patted the small space left for me. I liked the thought that we would have to snuggle up next to each other. I crawled in next to him and he held me close. Feeling safe and secure that Sam, at least, knew what he was doing, I fell asleep quickly.

About 1:30 a.m., I woke up to find that Sam was gone. I rolled over to look at the bedside clock and realized it was 7:30 in the evening in Ohio. I was glad we had plenty of time left for lots of sleep to make up for the night before and I snuggled back down in the bed. Then, because of Freya's hardwood floors, I could hear voices from downstairs. My chest and stomach lurched painfully. Were Blythe and her girls here?

I quietly got up and looked around in the dark for a weapon. I had noticed a walking cane in the wardrobe, an accessory for one of the Regency costumes. I had looked through them all before getting in the bed and decided the closet was a dress-up playhouse for adults.

I felt my way over to the wardrobe, pulled it open and found the cane. It felt solid in my hand, and I had no doubts that I would be able to use it to protect Sam or Freya or her kids if the situation required it. I pulled the door open as silently as I could and started down the stairs to where I could still hear the murmur of voices. As I reached the kitchen, I could see the glow of Freya's laptop and two figures sitting at it. I gripped the cane and held my breath so I could hear what they were saying.

"She doesn't know?" One voice was Freya's.

"Not yet." The other was my husband's.

Know *what*, I wondered? It was obvious they were referring to me. I tried to hold my breath, but as I put my foot slightly to the side, the floorboard of the hundreds-of-years-old house creaked. Both of them stiffened and slowly turned towards me.

I held up the cane. "It's me. I came to find Sam."

Sam relaxed and waved me over to join them. "Got a weapon, I see," he said.

This didn't seem the right thing to say in front of Freya. Wouldn't it make her suspicious?

"I was just curious what it was like to use one of these," I said with a shaky laugh. But I wasted no time. "So, what is it I don't know?"

Freya turned on a lamp. I could see she was still dressed in the clothes she'd been wearing when we arrived. I felt jealousy bubbling up inside me. *Had Sam wanted me to fall asleep so he could be alone with her? He had known exactly how to find her house and she had recognized his voice straight away. Were they secret friends or colleagues…or worse? What was the lie this time?*

Freya glanced at me and then at Sam. "I'll make us some tea."

Too disturbed by the secretiveness to play along, I said, "Sam would rather have coffee."

Sam chuckled nervously. "Tea sounds good." He gestured to the chair beside him. "Let's all sit down. I have more explaining to do."

This was exactly what I had been afraid of. I wasn't sure I could handle anymore revelations. "Just tell me quick. Is it good or bad?" Sam pulled out a chair for me while Freya made tea. I sat down, still holding the walking stick in my hand. It comforted me for some reason.

"I'll make it short," he said. "It's all good." I glared at him but said nothing.

"Freya is the one who originally recommended me for the job as an independent contractor. She was approached right after university for a position and once she'd proven herself capable in a job such as ours, they asked her for recommendations. She knew that I had similar talents and interests as she did, which is what made me such a great husband for you and her such a best friend to you. You balanced us both in a good way."

I knew he was trying to manipulate me with a compliment, but it *did* make me feel better. Freya and I had been best friends in university and we'd always said the reason why was because we were opposites who admired each other's skills and interests rather than being jealous or intimidated of each other. When I met Sam, I told her that he was the male version of her. It all made sense, but I still hated they'd kept this secret from me for so many years.

My mother was certainly right. I was either very naïve or had my head buried in the sand. Mother always meant that she thought

Sam was hiding something bad, but if Sam and Freya were being forthright with me now—and I could only trust and hope they were—then what they had been hiding had been for the good.

Together, they explained how they'd sometimes worked together over the years on assignments, but not very often since they had different skillsets. I asked Freya what she was good at and she said that she employed pharmaceuticals to help the good guys and outwit the bad guys. "So, my apothecary's shop…" I nodded yes and she continued. "That's my decoy of a sort. I *do* own and work at the shop and use the various medicines to take to medical conferences and teach doctors and pharmacists. That's what I tell my family, anyway. My mother-in-law comes to stay and helps take care of Arthur and the kids. Often, however, I'm actually on assignments for our company, like Sam."

I had a million questions. Like, do your kids and Arthur feel neglected, too? Did you miss their birthday parties? I bit my tongue—I really hoped that the "company" they worked for *was* truly helping the good guys.

Freya took a tin of biscuits from the cupboard.

"No thanks," I said frostily.

She set the tin on the table next to our cups of tea. "This is not what you think it is. This is a shipment of a new drug that I just received and haven't taken down to the shop yet." She opened the tin and pulled out a vial and syringe. I wondered if she was going to stab me with it and clutched my walking stick under the table. If she saw my obvious discomfort, she ignored it.

"One shot of this potion and the victim will immediately collapse and give all indications of being dead. The pulse stops, the heartbeat stops, breathing stops, movement stops, and the eyes roll back and stare. However, it's all temporary and not real. It can be used as a decoy to escape or to drop an attacker and buy some time."

I could tell she was proud of this magical potion, but the details didn't really interest me.

"We call it the Juliet drug," she said, "as in Romeo and Juliet. You know how she fakes dying at the end?"

"Really clever," I said sarcastically, but I did have one important question. I looked at Sam. "Do you know what we're doing tomorrow?"

I didn't know if we were hiding the information about Elizabeth from Freya or if she was in on it. I decided to keep the secret until Sam told me otherwise.

"Yes," he said, "after we wake up and drink our tea, we'll go to Freya's shop and she will squire us around Bath for a while. I can use her mobile or house phone to find out our next step. And now we should all really go to bed."

Freya got up to hug me, but I dodged her and followed Sam out of the room and back up the stairs. I kept the walking stick by my side of the bed just in case another secret was revealed in the next few hours and I needed a weapon.

I accosted Sam when he shut the bedroom door and climbed into bed beside me. "Am I supposed to believe that story?" Now the bed felt too small, and I wanted to move as far from him as possible.

"I'm really sorry, Marion, and I wish there was a better word to say than sorry. I didn't know what would happen when we got here. I wanted to make sure Freya wasn't working with Blythe. I'm not certain yet if she even knows about Elizabeth.

"All of us work on a need-to-know basis for our protection. We don't really think of it as lies or secrets. It's just the information we need to know at the time we need to know it. We work in the present tense. Otherwise, what others are doing is kind of none of our business."

He paused. "I realized I was treating you like that, too. I can see now how it began to really damage our marriage. I still want to protect you, though, and I think Freya does, too."

"So tomorrow we're going around Bath?" I asked. "What about Elizabeth?"

"I said that to throw Freya off, just in case. Actually, we'll leave first thing in the morning for Stratford-on-Avon. You told me there's a Shakespeare Festival going on which means it will be nice and packed with people. That is always safer."

He turned on his side to face me. "I went downstairs when I thought Freya was asleep, and I was able to reach my contact on the house phone before she heard me and came to the kitchen. I'll meet my friend in Stratford and drop off Elizabeth. This should be taken care of by noon tomorrow."

I closed my eyes and tried to stop worrying.

5

Festivals and Fancy Dress

Pink streaks of dawn through the lacy white curtains woke me, but within a minute of opening my eyes, the pink had turned to pale gray. "Good morning, beautiful," said Sam with a smile. He pulled me into his arms and began talking about the day's plans. He acted like this was a normal work day, and I guessed it *was* for him.

"Freya told me last night we should wear some of her costumes to blend in with the crowds today as we walk around," he said.

I corrected him. "Fancy dress, not costumes."

"Sure, okay, whatever they're called. Apparently, there are several parades and Jane Austen events today. I assume that Blythe has tracked us here by now so getting to Stratford undetected is paramount."

"How are we going to get away from Freya without her suspecting us?"

"I have an idea for that. Just follow my lead like you did last night."

"That means I'm going to look ridiculous again."

He ignored me and carried on. "We need to stay tech-free for now and stay off the grid as far as credit and bank cards are concerned because that's the easiest way for Blythe to trace us. Freya said she can lend us some cash and other supplies. She'll get reimbursed for it all as a business expense."

I rolled my eyes at his ease in talking about this like it was a business lunch with some computer salesman, but his matter-of-fact manner did reassure me that he and Freya knew what they were doing, even though they didn't want *me* to know what they were doing. But something still bugged me. "How do we know Freya is still working with you and hasn't gone over to the dark side like Blythe?"

Sam sat up in the bed. "We don't know for certain yet. She'll know I used her house phone to make the contact, so we'll know whose side she's on by noon. I've gotten pretty good at reading people over the years and I think she's still all right. But being cautious is always good."

We heard a soft knock on the door. Sam went into the en-suite and nodded at me to answer it. When I opened it, Tilly was standing there in her navy and burgundy school uniform. Just adorable.

"Good morning, Mrs. Martin," she said. "Mummy told me not to wake you, but I wanted to say good-bye before I go to school."

"That's all right. I'm glad you did." I leaned over to give her a hug. "Your mother and I have been friends for a long time, and I'm really happy to finally see where she lives and to meet you."

"Daddy comes home on the four o'clock train today. Will you still be here to see him?" she asked.

"I'm not sure yet. Remember the airline lost our luggage? If they find it, we may have to go to London to get it or they may send it here. I'll be wearing your mother's jumper again today."

"I have to go now but I hope you're still here when James and I get home from school."

We hugged again before she disappeared downstairs. Sam called to me when I closed the bedroom door. "What was that all about?"

"Just sweet girl talk with Tilly," I said.

He put on a complicated black suit with long black boots and a top hat. "I hate to bring this up," he said, "but sometimes in our business we get information we need from children. Did you tell Tilly anything that would let Freya know our real plans?"

I crossed my arms. "As a matter of fact, I didn't. I told her we might have to go to London if the airline finds our luggage."

"That was pretty good," he said, handing me a hanger with a lovely pale pink ball gown. "Here, how about wearing this?"

My heart admittedly leapt a little in excitement about getting to wear such fun clothes. I started to take the dress, but then paused. "Sam," I said, "just as a precaution until we drop off Elizabeth, let's switch out our clothes. We'll go downstairs so everyone can see us, and then when they leave for school, we can run back upstairs and change into something different. That way if Freya tells Blythe or whomever that we're wearing pink and black, we'll be able to throw them off the trail a bit."

Sam looked at me in surprise. "That's a good idea. Done."

I had to help Sam with some buttons and ties, but when he was done dressing, he looked absolutely dashing. Why don't we dress like this anymore? I put on the pink dress with white gloves and a pink bonnet and Sam buttoned me up the back.

"There's an incredible number of buttons back here," he said. "No wonder they had servants to dress them."

"Hurry, or they'll be gone," I said.

When I caught our reflection in the hall mirror, I couldn't help smiling. We did look quite nice. Too bad we couldn't really go to a ball and dance our worries away.

We made our grand entrance into the kitchen where James and Tilly were putting on their school rucksacks. It is un-American of me, I know, but I think girls in skirts and knee socks and boys in suits and ties look so much better than the scruffy jeans and t-shirts my sons wore.

"Mrs. Martin, you look gorgeous," Tilly gushed. "Mummy, why can't we go to the festival, too?"

James chimed in. "Right, Mummy. Why are we going to school when we have house guests?"

Freya smiled and pointed toward the stairs. "You know you are going with your school tomorrow. Today is for the adults. Head downstairs and into the car." She turned back to us. "I'll do the school run, stop off for coffee, and be back as quickly as possible. Help yourself to tea, toast, whatever you can find. You both do look fabulous. The pink is gorgeous on you, Marion."

"All thanks to you," I said. "See you soon."

As the door shut downstairs, Sam muttered, "Not too quickly, I hope. Come on, Marion, let's get changed and out of here before she gets back."

My heart raced again as we rushed upstairs to change into different fancy dress. I really liked the pink dress and wished I could keep it on. I looked through the wardrobe to see if anything else would look as good on me and skipped over a pale green and peach dress. It would look ghastly with my brown hair and eyes. Sam yelled, "Hurry up!" and I jumped. He was right. This was not a fashion shoot.

I spied a sprigged eggshell-blue dress on a hanger with a ruffled cap. It would look pretty on me *and* hide my face and hair. Perfect. Sam and I quickly helped each other unbutton and untie and change. I gasped with delight as Sam dressed in a scarlet and royal blue

British uniform and became Mr. Wickam. This would have been so much fun if only we had been there on holiday.

Sam seemed moved by my attire too. "Mrs. Martin, may I have the honor of escorting you to the train station and then to visit our esteemed friend, William Shakespeare?"

"My pleasure," I replied and took his proffered arm. "You *do* know Shakespeare died two hundred years before Jane Austen."

"Details, details, my love...now let's go."

We glided down Freya's stairs and exited her front door. I stopped and glanced at Sam. "Wait just a minute."

I ran back up the flight to the kitchen and grabbed the biscuit tin with Freya's new potion. I didn't have an immediate idea for it, but it gave me a satisfied rush to do something secret myself. I ran my hand across her counter sending everything to the floor and then grabbed her laptop and dropped it on the floor. It landed with an even more satisfying crash.

Sam called up the stairs. "What's going on? Are you all right?"

"Yes, I'm coming. It's fine."

I knocked over two of the chairs for good measure and ran back downstairs in a quite unladylike manner. When I reached the floor, I took his arm again. My heart was beating quickly, but I felt invigorated.

Sam hurried toward the train station. "What was going on up there?"

"I had the idea to make Freya think we'd had an encounter with Blythe, so I kind of messed up her kitchen to throw her off our track."

Sam glanced sideways at me, but I lowered my head under the bonnet so he couldn't see my blushing face. The bonnet was convenient in many ways.

"Freya has only been my colleague at the company," he said, "and was very helpful last night. I know you are special to her. We are taking precautions, but I don't suspect her of collaborating with Blythe at this point."

"That's great," I said. "Then we don't need to worry about anything. We'll just sneak back to the train station, ride to Stratford-upon-Avon, and drop off Elizabeth. Easy peasy."

A large group of similarly-dressed Regency ladies and gentlemen were in the middle of the street square and were partnering off into couples. Musicians were on the sidewalk, and a woman dressed in a lavender dress with a matching feather in the curls of her chignon was holding a microphone and giving instructions. I slowed and watched.

"Keep moving," Sam murmured.

"I thought you said to blend into the crowd."

The lavender-feathered lady spotted us and said through her microphone, "Mr. Wickam and Miss Blue, please join this set of six." She gestured to three couples standing in two rows. The men were on one side and faced the ladies across from them.

"Please?" I begged. Sam sighed and joined the line of men as I joined the ladies, and we faced one another.

"Good," said Miss Lavender. "Now we shall begin. Ladies, step forward, one, two, three…and curtsy, four, five, six. Gentlemen, bow…one, two, three…and kiss your lady's hand…four, five, six."

I needed to get rid of the biscuit tin, so I emptied its contents into my dainty embroidered bag and threw the tin into the nearest rubbish bin.

"Miss Blue, we're waiting," rebuked Miss Lavender.

"Sorry, madam," I said and rejoined the line as our instructor continued walking us through the steps of the period dance. I was in Jane Austen heaven.

"Now with the music, please," commanded Miss Lavender.

The musicians, who were attired brilliantly in black riding trousers with white long socks, white shirts, and black vests, started playing a lovely waltz, and Miss Lavender talked us through the steps again. "Excellent!" she said as we finished bowing, twirling, spinning, and gracefully sashaying. "Let's do it once more with the music, and then we'll be ready for the exhibition at the Assembly Rooms."

We effortlessly performed the dance again to the live music, smiling, eyes locked on our partners, long dresses swishing. The demure dance was pure romance. The music was almost done when Sam jerked my arm.

"Let's go. Keep your head turned towards me."

I knew he must have seen something, and I immediately obeyed his directions. We walked briskly away from the dancers although my adrenaline wanted me to run.

"What did you see?" I whispered.

"A black cab with a pony-tailed driver. It might not be Blythe, but let's assume it is," he said. I couldn't help wondering if Blythe had traced us or if Freya had told her where we were. Before I could voice my thoughts, Sam said, "There she is! This way."

We turned away from the train station onto York Street. "She's driving by the train station," I said. "That's where she expects us to go."

He charged ahead. "What about another boating adventure?"

I tried to look straight ahead, but it was hard for me to see. Maybe the bonnet wasn't so great after all.

The sounds of sea birds alerted me that we were near the river Avon, and Sam stopped at a sign that read Bath Boats and Private Tours. "Wait here so they won't remember seeing two of us," he said.

I tried to make myself as inconspicuous as possible by looking in a shop window with beautiful umbrellas of all colours and designs. Sam came back out and ducked his head, leaning against the shop window. I was annoyed because he had blocked my view of a stately black umbrella with a brass parrot head on the handle. It was very Mary Poppinish.

"I hired a narrow boat. We could take it all the way to Stratford-on-Avon, but it will be too slow for us to make our noon appointment. So, we'll ride the boat for a bit, and then change at the next town with a car hire or train station. We can't risk a run-in with Blythe here in Bath since, for now, we have to suspect that Freya is her backup."

"How can you bear not knowing if your colleagues are for or against you?" I asked.

"None of this has happened to me before. I'm sort of feeling my way through it. I just don't want to wrongly suspect someone," he answered.

I took Sam's arm again in renewed satisfaction that he was one of the good guys, and we glided down the boat ramp to a cheerfully painted wooden boat with the name *Tea Time* painted on its side.

The boats were long and narrow so that two boats could pass one another on the narrow man-made canals of England. Originally used for shipping, now they were used for pleasure. I once read a book about a couple who had converted their canal boat into a houseboat and boated all over England for a year. It seemed romantic in the book, but as the captain greeted us and remarked on what a nice couple we made in our fancy dress, I felt only panic. I wanted the slow-moving boat to move as quickly as possible out of Bath.

"It's a sunny day. Best enjoy it now because it's sure to rain soon," said the captain, whose embroidered nametag read "Captain Jack."

"I think we'll go inside and watch from there," said Sam.

Captain Jack looked surprised that we didn't want to take advantage of the bright sunlight. "Suit yourself," he said.

Sam lowered his head to get through the doorway, and we left the captain on the deck. Inside was a small sitting room complete with a miniature sofa, table, and two chairs just the right size for the compact space. "We should change and hide or sink our costumes," said Sam.

"Fancy dress," I said under my breath.

I knew he was right, but I felt sad about shedding my pretty frock for the wrinkled black trousers and brown jumper Sam had been carrying in a leather satchel belonging to Freya's husband. Before we could start the unbuttoning process, though, Captain Jack knocked on the door and poked his head in.

"It will take us about an hour to get to the next landing dock. Your trip includes tea time. We have sandwiches, scones, and—of course—clotted cream and strawberry jam. Would you be wanting to eat now or in half an hour?"

We hadn't eaten breakfast and tea time sounded delicious. I'd worked up an appetite after dancing. "What do you think, Sam? Now or later?"

"Now sounds good, thank you," said Sam.

The captain grimaced. "We have a slight problem, but I think it easily remedied. My first mate—that's me wife—couldn't help me today. She says she had an appointment, but I think that means she's getting her hair done. She usually takes care of preparing the tea while I steer the boat."

"We can help you," I said and clapped my hands together like Tilly would probably do.

"Thank you, Madam. If you can put the kettle on, my wife put everything you'll need on a tray on the counter, and the rest is in that wee fridge there."

I put the kettle on to boil. The captain tipped his cap, nodded, and went back to the deck.

"You sit there and relax and let me serve you," I said to Sam, feeling like a real lady from the 1700s.

"My pleasure, my dear."

Sam sat in the "wee" chair at the table which meant he had to stretch his long legs over half the sitting room. I bustled around, setting the table. The tray was painted white and the tea cups and saucers were a fun mishmash of pastel flowers. Some of the china was chipped but that added to the endearment of it all. "There are lumps of sugar in the sugar bowl," I exclaimed.

"Exciting," said Sam, a touch of tease in his tone.

I unwrapped a plate of scones with currants. Then, as the captain had promised, I found sliced sandwiches with no crusts in the mini fridge and brought those over to the table. There were dear little pots of strawberry jam, golden clotted cream, and a tiny pitcher of milk. A variety of wildflowers were perched in the middle of the table. I blessed the first mate and sent a silent prayer that his wife's hair would turn out beautifully.

"I think the cutlery is real silver!" I said.

A hint of a smile appeared on Sam's face. "The things that get you excited," he said, shaking his head and piling sandwiches on his dainty pink-and-blue-flowered china plate. The kettle whistled, and I brought it over to the table to fill the teapot that already had English Breakfast tea bags in it.

"Is this right?" asked Sam as he lifted his teacup and saucer with a raised pinky.

"Perfect," I said, happy he was playing along with me.

We tasted everything and used up all the clotted cream, piling it high on the split scones.

"Why don't we have this in America?" I asked.

I paused and changed the subject. "Can I ask you a question?"

Sam took a bite of scone and squinted at me. "About clotted cream?"

"No, silly. About Elizabeth."

"Ask away, but remember if I can't tell you something, it's for your protection."

"I know, I know. What I don't understand is what exactly we're dropping off? Is it intellectual property or actually a thing, because you don't have anything with you unless it's in your shoe. Or do you have to tell somebody where you hid something?"

A horn sounded and we both jumped. Sam went to the window to look out. "We're passing another boat." He turned back to face me and said, "Marion, I'm sorry, I just can't explain. After this is all done, I will, I promise."

Captain Jack competently steered us through, and our tea party was over. "We need to change," I said.

Sam nodded, spun me around so my back was to him, and started unbuttoning me. As I shed my lovely clothes, my ladylike demeanor disappeared, too, and I dressed in neutral practicality. "Where should we hide these?" I asked.

"I don't think we need to worry about that now. We can just leave them on the boat. I want to get my bearings so when we get to the next landing I'll know exactly where to go to get a car or train. I'll ask the captain in a roundabout way."

Sam put on brown trousers with a black dress shirt. He looked nice, but not nearly as dashing as he had in the Wickam attire. I folded our beautiful clothes and laid them neatly out of sight in the tiny loo.

Then I went to the window to see the scenery. The boat continued slowly down the Avon. As I looked through the window, my eyes feasted on the bowers of flowers, the riverbank, and buildings and homes outside of Bath. I turned back to look where we'd been and leaning over a charming deck rail, I saw three women dressed in black, sporting bad-lady ponytails and sunglasses, and pointing towards our boat.

6

Something Wicked This Way Comes

"**S**am! They see us!"

He rushed over and joined me to look out the window. "Ok, Plan B," he replied calmly.

I mumbled under my breath. "I think we're on Plan W."

"They'll have to get on a boat to follow us or they might have asked at the dock or boat rental where we're going and are driving to follow us along the way," he said. "Either way, the faster we move, the better."

Sam went outside, and I noticed he was careful to stand in a way that would block Blythe's view. He spoke to the captain, but I couldn't hear him over the sound of the engine. Captain Jack shook his head, and I had the feeling this old boat couldn't go any faster. Swimming to Stratford might be faster. I peered through the back window again to see if I could still see the ponytails, but they were out of sight.

I wanted to get to Stratford and meet the contact, but waiting for Sam to come back inside gave me a minute for a slew of my unanswered questions to return.

Did Freya rat us out or was she still our friend? What did she think about what I did to her kitchen? I hoped she would clean up the mess before the kids got home and were frightened. It wasn't their fault if their mother was a double-agent.

Then I wondered again about Elizabeth. Where was Sam keeping her? Blythe would have had him searched in jail. She'd taken everything out of our room, after all. Where could he have had time to hide her? For all I knew, he could have hidden her months before in another country. Maybe even at our house.

That immediately made me think of our kids. Oh, God, I missed Bear and hoped he was doing all right with my mom. I still ached every day over William, but even though the pain was familiar, I realized I had been distracted from it with all the escaping and hiding we'd been doing. I didn't know if that was good or bad.

Sam came back and confirmed that the boat couldn't go any faster. "It will take us hours to get to Stratford and we don't have hours. We are only ten minutes away from the next landing, but I don't know if that gives us enough time to spare before Blythe and her friends catch up with us."

He slammed his hand on the counter top and rattled our dirty dishes. "We *have* to meet my friend in Stratford," he said.

I shuddered. It was the first time I'd seen him angry or agitated during this entire experience. "What if we risk getting off at the next town and catch a bus or train or taxi?"

"We can do that, but Blythe will most likely be there waiting for us. She'll be following us all the way looking for an opportunity to waylay us."

"What about backtracking? Since Blythe's left Bath, what if we jump ship now and go back to Bath? We can probably get back on the train without her seeing us."

Sam shook his head. "In Bath, there's still the Freya wild card. She may be watching for us, too."

I looked through the front window and saw we were approaching a lovely arched bridge adorned with flowers and an idea came to me. "Can you tell Captain Jack that we're going to rest so he won't disturb us? Then he won't know we've left. We can jump off the front of the boat and climb up the bank. Maybe we'll find a bike or horse to ride into town."

That I was giving directions was a role reversal and I felt stronger being the one making a decision. The only way for us to get off the boat without Captain Jack noticing was to go out the front and slip off the side, hoping he was looking in a different direction. I was sure Sam could jump far enough and quietly enough, and I prayed that I could too.

Sam thought for a moment. "Let's do it," he said and went back to talk to Captain Jack. When he returned, I opened the door as narrowly as possible, and motioned for him to go first. He crawled through and I followed. I scraped my knee on the deck, but I couldn't be bothered about it.

Sam slipped over the side, rose to the surface away from the boat and beckoned for me to come in the murky water. The *Tea Time* passed under the bridge and I took a breath and prepared to launch myself from the boat. Sam waved his arm faster, a sign that he'd seen something on the bridge.

The cold water sent a shock through me, and I panicked as the weight of my clothes pulled me down, but Sam's strong hand reached down and pulled me up. Once my head was above water again, I looked at the bridge. Sure enough, there was Blythe leaning over the railing and looking down at our boat.

"Ahoy, there!" she called down to the captain. "I have some

friends on your boat. Can you give them this, please, when they disembark?"

I couldn't hear the captain's reply, but she called out, "Thank you," and tossed something over the bridge.

Was it a bomb? I didn't want anything bad to happen to the *Tea Time* or its captain. "Duck," Sam instructed, and he took a deep breath and went underwater. I followed suit and braced myself for an explosion. I swam as best I could towards Sam and we came up for air beneath the bridge. The narrow boat continued on undisturbed.

"Wait to make sure she's gone," he whispered, and I nodded. For a few cold silent minutes, we paddled in place while Sam held onto a groove in the bridge and I held onto him.

Finally, he spoke again. "It should be all right for us to get out now," he said, and we struggled against the current. When we reached the bank, I asked Sam what he thought Blythe had thrown on the boat.

"I'm pretty sure she threw another one of her tracking devices, probably the red phone. The captain wouldn't be suspicious of that."

"She's tracking us," I wailed.

"Thanks to you, she's tracking the *boat*," Sam corrected. "One thing in our favor is that she wants us alive for now, so I doubt she'd use a bomb. That's not really the company style."

I slipped in the mud, and my shoes suctioned off. I was miserable.

"Sorry, I'm not familiar with your company's policies," I said, pouting. Sam ignored the comment.

"Let's get to the closest town and on the quickest transport we can find to Stratford. We're going to be late." He made it sound like we were running behind for a dentist appointment and I grumbled inside as I struggled up the bank in my wet clothes.

We followed a path that led to what appeared to be civilization, but there were no signs for a train station. I scanned the street and saw a small red and white car with a taxi sign on top.

"There's a cab," I said, thankful it wasn't black. Sam flagged it down, but when the driver saw our dripping clothes, he refused to take us.

"Give us something we can sit on, and we'll pay you double," said Sam.

The driver looked us over. "Double and a half. Stratford's a long way from here."

"Get us there in half the time and I'll pay you triple."

"Deal," said the cabbie, and he pulled a tarp out of his trunk and spread it across the back. We carefully slid in on top of it.

I decided it was better to close my eyes as the driver raced on the wrong side of the road in the narrowest of lanes. I leaned against Sam's warm shoulder. But not for long. It occurred to me what day it was and I sat up with a jerk.

"What's wrong?" asked Sam.

"Well, besides the obvious, we were supposed to be in London today. I had a surprise for you. I got us tickets to see *Lés Mis*. Surprise!" I pretended to hand him a present.

"Thank you, I love it. That was a great surprise. We can still make the theatre, though. We'll go see a Shakespeare play instead."

"It's a date," I said and closed my eyes again.

I must have dozed off, because I woke up to Sam talking to our driver. "You can drop us in front of Shakespeare's house."

When we got out of the car, we were still a wet mess. I couldn't help laughing at my husband. His hair was almost dry, but it was sticking up in the back and his clothes were rumpled. He was a far sight from the debonair gentleman I had danced with earlier.

"What are *you* laughing at?" he said, as he handed the driver a wad of wet bank notes.

He looped the leather satchel sideways over his shirt and held out his hand to me. "I'm sure I look as funny as you do," I said ruefully.

Sam smiled and shook his head. "No, my dear, you look as beautiful as always." He bowed with a flourish. "Shakespeare's house awaits you, Mrs. Martin."

The black-and-tan half-timbered wattle and daub home stood out on Henley Street amongst the smaller buildings around it. A crowd of tourists queued up to get tickets. Many were dressed in Elizabethan fancy dress and tourists posed for pictures with them. We anxiously waited in line, but it moved quickly.

Sam bought two tickets in cash and we went inside the museum attached to Shakespeare's place of birth and childhood. The English woman at the ticket counter was apparently too polite to comment on our wet attire. As we walked away from the counter, I whispered to Sam. "Where are we meeting your friend?"

He didn't answer but hurried us past crowds of tourists watching a video about the famous playwright and went out into an English garden complete with roses and a picket fence, where actors dressed in Shakespearean garb were acting out scenes. I heard one of my favourite Romeo and Juliet passages, and recited along with the man attired in a royal blue velvet shirt and lighter blue stockings.

"Two households,
both alike in dignity,
in fair Verona,
where we lay our scene,
from ancient grudge break to new mutiny,
where civil blood makes civil hands unclean."

Sam grinned at me. "Show off," he said. "I wish we were here for fun, but after today, I can make it up to you." It was an off-repeated phrase Sam had used over the years when he'd missed a birthday party or soccer game or was late to a recital. Once he'd even been a no-show for a surprise party for me that he'd planned. I guess the surprise for me was that he wasn't there.

My stomach roiled. Now I knew why he'd missed a lot of our family activities and at least, this time, I was with him on one of his merry adventures. I have to admit that "England Adventure" was a nicer way of thinking of what was happening than "Date with Death."

I took a calming breath and smiled at him in a hopefully reassuring way. Maybe he really believed everything would be fine soon. I wasn't so sure. A puzzled expression appeared on Sam's face. "I thought we'd have seen him by now," he said in a low voice. "Let's go inside the house."

I nodded, and we followed the crowds into the small quaint home in which Shakespeare had grown up. Fancy-dressed docents were in every room telling the visitors what interesting tidbits happened in each room. One asked us if we wanted to try on the Shakespeare clothes that were hanging on pegs in the low ceiling room with a fireplace. "You can even act out some of the parts. We have cards that you can read from," she explained.

"That sounds like fun, but I don't think we have time," I replied.

"Oh, let's do it," Sam said. "It will be fun."

I was confused, but I followed his lead. "Okay," I said. Shrugging, I put a bonnet over my still damp hair and tied a blue velvet cloak over my still damp clothes while Sam put on a black cloak and a felt cap. He pushed my hair under the bonnet and laughed, saying that my earrings didn't quite look the part.

"You should probably take them off for a few minutes while we play *Romeo and Juliet*."

I didn't want to bother unscrewing my new earrings for the few minutes I was sure we would only be able to act our scene, but Sam had his hand out, so I started unscrewing the left one. They had certainly stayed on just fine through a spate of disasters.

The docent stopped me with her hand and told us it was show time. She led us back outside to the garden, handed us some index cards. "*I* will be Macbeth. Your ladyship will play Lady Macbeth, and you, sir, will play Duncan. Stick to the script and…all's well that ends well," she said, smiling. I was tickled by her joke, but I doubted Sam noticed the Shakespearean mix ups.

The woman put on a king's crown and royal robes and took up a dagger from a trunk of props. I was amazed at how real it looked. She handed me a queen's crown and gave me huge gaudy earrings. I took off the bonnet and unscrewed the other earring and handed it to Sam for safekeeping. I was so excited to live out a Shakespeare dream that I didn't even have stage fright. I was performing in The Bard's garden!

A town crier rang a bell and called out, "Hear ye, hear ye! Please gather around to watch a scene from *Macbeth*. Silence your phones, but pictures and videos are permitted. Hear ye, hear ye!"

Macbeth, who was being played by a woman—another inside joke since the parts of women were played by men in Shakespeare's day—handed Sam and me our prompt cards and I laid the gaudy earrings on a side table. I was starting to enjoy myself. She—or he—said, "Follow my lead."

From somewhere in the crowd of people gathering around to watch us, I heard the familiar ringtone of an old house phone. I froze. "She's here," I said to Sam. "I hear the red phone."

Sam didn't move. "The show must go on," he said in a low voice. "We've got to make this contact. Follow the script...and follow me."

I looked around the crowded garden for Blythe or the other women, but no one looked familiar. Then, I heard the ring tone again. A tattooed man in black leather trousers and cap complained loudly. "Come on, he said to silence our phones. Can't we enjoy the show?"

A man in a baseball cap and t-shirt took his black mobile out of his pocket and silenced it. "Whoops, my bad," he said.

What a relief. I was too jumpy. I supposed that Blythe was still on the River Avon.

Our docent smiled and said, "Ready?"

We nodded in response and followed her onto the lawn with our cue cards. She carried the dagger.

"Where are Lady Macbeth's earrings, love?" she asked me.

"I'm sorry, I didn't have time to put them on. They're still on the table back there. Should I get them?"

"You have time. They really make the outfit. I have a long monologue first so you can finish dressing while I'm doing that."

I pushed the left earring through my ear while the docent began reciting the first lines of her part as Macbeth. Too bad we weren't taking pictures of all our outfit changes. I guessed spies didn't really post on Facebook or Instagram.

Macbeth's voice rose a little and she turned toward my husband. "Duncan, something wicked this way comes." I frowned. *That* wasn't part of her script. It was one of the witch's lines, but it wasn't in the scene we were doing. It was only then that I realized the docent was our contact. She was warning Sam that we'd been infiltrated.

Standing on my tiptoes to see over the tourists holding up their cell phones, I saw that someone wicked was indeed coming. Blythe was pushing her way through the crowd.

How did she know to find us at Shakespeare's house, unless she already knew who the contact was? I guessed they all worked together and knew one another. All my doubts came crashing down again. All I knew to do was to cause a distraction.

Blythe began wrestling with the docent and I surmised that Sam had already given Elizabeth to the docent while they were on the stage together. I assumed they'd sent me back to get the earrings so I wouldn't see the exchange.

Rather than calling the police, the duped audience was clapping unknowingly at a *real* fight scene. I picked up one of the prop chairs, hoping it wasn't a valuable antique, and flung it at Blythe. She easily ducked. Sam turned to me. "Lady Macbeth, stay out of this. Go back inside, and I will meet you out front on the street."

I couldn't bear to leave him with this vile woman, but I had no fighting skills. Macbeth took out her dagger and Blythe did some sort of karate maneuver and the dagger flew away and onto the ground. The crowd backed away and applauded again.

Sam, Blythe, and Macbeth all dove for the knife and Mr. Tattoo started yelling, "Security! Security!" as a little boy gleefully ran to join the fray. Sam picked up the boy and shoved him safely back to the crowd, which allowed Blythe to get to the dagger. Then, while Sam's back was turned, Blythe struck at Macbeth, who crumpled onto the grass.

Now the crowd was really confused because the blood on the ground looked real. Someone screamed and the crowd scattered. Blythe, still holding the bloody knife, lunged toward Sam, and he took off through the crowd towards the entrance.

I too ran back inside the four-hundred-year-old home and pushed my way to the front room. A window—which only the wealthy could afford back in the day—was cracked open, and a display of leather gloves and goods that Shakespeare's father made were lying across the sill. Praying for forgiveness for my irreverence, I brushed the carefully-preserved antiques onto the floor and pushed on the window.

"Oy! You can't do that! What do you think you're doing?" shouted a docent in a wheelchair in the front room.

I mumbled, "Sorry," as I squeezed my way through the narrow space and out a window for the second time in one day. My crown fell off, and Sam—who was already out front—raced to the window, and pulled me out.

"We meet again," he said.

"What's going on? I don't understand. Did you do it? Is she dead?" I started to cry. This was just too much. Daggers, crowns, Duncan, destroying property, and now, being rude to the disabled.

"Let's go," he said.

I tried to pull away from him. "I'm not going anywhere with you."

Police cars and an ambulance roared by us with screaming sirens and stopped in the front of the museum.

"We've got to get out of here, Marion," he said, and hailed a taxi that was driving by. "Get in," he said, and half shoved me into the car. He put his hand on my head to protect it like a police officer would do to a criminal.

"I don't know if it's safe," I wailed.

An Indian man dressed in a purple turban asked us where we needed to go. "To London, please, to Heathrow," said Sam, as he strapped my seatbelt over my body.

"To Heathrow airport in London? That will cost you."

"I understand," said Sam, "I have British pound sterling to pay you."

108

"I'll need two hundred up front."

Sam shoved pound notes through the front window and demanded the cabbie start driving. The cash tactic was successful again and we pulled away.

Sam leaned forward and closed the partition to the front seat. "Well, that didn't go quite as planned." He pulled off his Duncan cloak and wig.

I crossed my arms resolutely. "I'm not getting out of this taxi until you explain what happened back there. I warn you, Sam. I will start screaming if you don't start talking."

"I'm not sure," he finally said with a sigh, "but Macbeth definitely got hurt. I'm not sure how serious it is, but she'll be taken to hospital. She knows what she signed up for. It's part of the job."

"Well, I'm not sure *I* know what I signed up for." I struggled to take off my cloak, which was wrapped around the seat belt. Tears ran down my face.

"Here, let me help you," said Sam as he unbuckled and gallantly unwrapped me. Then he used the cloak to wipe my tears.

He glanced at the front seat. "We have to be quiet. Obviously, there are eyes and ears everywhere, but I'll tell you what I know." He looked at me and then back at the driver. "Blythe got there before I had an opportunity to get rid of Elizabeth and now that particular contact of mine is exposed, assuming she's still alive."

He sighed and leaned across me to buckle me in again. "That's the down side of this job. Sometimes good people get hurt."

I caught his hand and turned to look him in the eyes. "Is it worth it, Sam? Tell me the truth. Is it worth it?"

He nodded with a firm resolve. "It *is*, Marion, it is."

I leaned back in the seat. "Well, then, what do we do now? Where are we flying?"

Sam held onto my hand and leaned back in the seat. "Part of my holiday plan for us was two weeks in Paris. So, let's go now. We can see the Eiffel Tower. It will be beautiful and crowded, and I can borrow someone's phone. I have another friend there."

He dug in his pocket and handed me the brown gemstone earrings. "Meanwhile, here," he said. "You can put these back on." I carefully inserted them into my ears and screwed them back on.

Sam leaned his head back and closed his eyes. "Let's rest while we can."

I sighed, mostly in frustration, but my heart wasn't racing anymore. A sliver of sunshine peeped through the gray clouds, and after months of Sam sometimes drinking himself to sleep and my dependence on sleeping pills to dull the pain, I was beginning to think maybe there was a blessing in being too tired to think.

Our driver turned onto the M4 motorway and the scenery looked like just another boring interstate. Sam's body relaxed into sleep and I had no choice but to shut my eyes, too.

7

Motives

O ur taxi driver coughed, and I raised up and glanced out the window. The sun was truly shining now and gave the afternoon a golden glow.

We were still on the motorway. Traffic was more congested, so I assumed we were getting close to the airport.

Sam leaned over and kissed me gently on the lips. "It's incredible to have your company on a work trip. I should have been taking you with me all along."

I supposed he was trying to cheer me up, but tears welled up in my eyes. The adrenaline rush of the past few days was now gone, and I just wanted to cry and sleep and wake up at home.

He wrapped his arms around me. "Mar, babe. I know, I know. You've been great. Amazing. You acted in an authentic Shakespeare play!"

Pouting, I mumbled into his arm. "Not really. I never got to say any of my lines, because Macbeth was murdered." I actually wanted to laugh, but I wasn't quite ready to stop crying.

"Isn't that what happens in the play?" asked Sam.

"No. In the play, *Duncan* dies, not Macbeth. It's all wrong. Everything's wrong. I can't do this anymore. I don't want to. I didn't know it would get this bad."

Sam lowered his voice. "Marion, it's worse than you know. I need to tell you the whole truth."

I pulled away from him. I didn't care anymore. I was too tired and scared to care about the rest of the story.

"Just let Blythe have it. Just give Elizabeth to her. How bad can it be?"

He pulled me back and whispered into my hair. "Bad. Very bad."

I stiffened. My intuition was telling me I would not enjoy hearing what he had to say next.

"What I've told you is the truth, but there's more," he whispered. "It's about William."

I jerked away from him. "What do you mean?"

"I think…no, I *know* that Blythe had something to do with the car crash."

I stared at my husband, aghast. "No," I said, "I'm the only one who had something to do with the car crash. I was driving. It was me. It was *my* fault that I ran off the road into the tree." I broke down into sobs, guilty sobs I'd shed in buckets over the past year.

Sam waited until my convulsions stopped. "No, honey," he said gently. "It *wasn't* your fault. That's what I'm trying to tell you. Blythe was in Lincoln on the day of the accident."

"What in the world are you talking about?"

"Before Freya discovered me in the kitchen the other night, I was on her computer trying to find out where Blythe was the day of the crash. I found evidence of flights, hotels, even a car she rented at the airport. I'm telling you that Blythe was there the day the crash happened, and I don't think it was a coincidence."

"Why would *she* have been in Lincoln?"

Sam shrugged. "That's the thing that's suspicious. I'm not a hundred percent sure but I know that Blythe was contacted by the… the…Dark Side…and she was pressuring me to turn sides with her. There was…is…a lot of money involved. And, as I'm sure you've guessed—or, at least, your mother has—Blythe was interested in having more than a working relationship with me."

I slid further away from my husband. I had known it. Mom had known it too.

"I still don't see what this has to do with William." As I said my son's name, I started to shake, and memories flooded my brain.

William, my firstborn son, was long, thin and lanky, built like his father, the opposite of his younger brother's husky build. When he was little, he'd loved to snuggle close to hear me read, and when he started reading on his own at a rather young age, he devoured books.

He was never difficult. The most rebellious he ever got was to refuse to wear a silly Christmas sweater his grandmother knitted him. I made him wear it on Christmas Day, but after that he said he lost it. I found it under a pile of clothes in his drawer after he died and I held it and cried and cried, because it was the only time he ever pushed back at what I told him to do.

He was my positive son, the one who would overlook and defend his dad's absences and broken promises. William helped me not give up on Sam—they looked so much alike that seeing Sam helped me feel like I had a part of Wills with me.

"Mom, relax. It's not a big deal about the party. I'm happy that all my friends are coming, and we can swim and play and eat junk food and sodas. You and Dad would just be talking to

the other grown-ups while we're swimming anyway," Wills said once when Sam called him to wish him an early thirteenth birthday and let him know that his business trip was taking longer than expected.

"Dad said he'd bring me back a gift from Germany. He always brings us the coolest stuff. Just relax, Mom. I'm not going to be scarred for life or anything. It's just a swim party," and he hugged me and tried to lift me up.

"OK," I said, laughing. "As long as you promise not to send us a bill for therapy when you grow up. Put me down. You'll drop me!"

He didn't drop me, and he only got taller and stronger. He made good grades and teachers and the other kids liked him. He was smart, but not in a nerdy way, even though Bear always teased him about being one.

They would yell back and forth and roughhouse, but it was all in fun. The kids had gotten used to Sam being gone—it was normal to them. The only thing that concerned them was our relationship—several of their friends' parents had divorced.

"You and Dad aren't getting a divorce, are you?" William asked me once when I was driving him home from soccer practice.

"No. Why are you asking that?" I said.

"Well, when Dad was home last week and he brought us those t-shirts from Brazil, you acted mad at him. Brandon said his mom started acting like that to his dad, getting mad at dumb stuff. Then his dad moved out, and they got a divorce."

"No honey, we aren't getting a divorce. When your dad gets back home from a long trip I don't know how to act sometimes. I'm sorry. Thanks for telling me. I can see why it's confusing." I reached over and patted his hand in reassurance.

"Want to stop at Dairy Queen for a happy hour blizzard?" I said to change the subject.

"Sure!"

Together Wills and I had deflected comments from Mom to keep everything positive. It worked so well, I believed it myself, even though Mom still harped about my naivete and ostrich-like tendency to avoid the truth.

I knew Wills would want me to listen to Sam now, so I took a deep breath, and to honor my son, I turned towards my husband and resolved to hear him out.

Sam was almost frantic. "Marion, like I told you before, I turned Blythe down absolutely. You have to believe me or nothing else I say will matter."

"I believe you," I said…and I did.

"Blythe was mad, and I think embarrassed, but her motivation was then, and still is, power and greed. She wants me to help her, and because I refused, I am a security risk for her. I have what I need to turn her in and to stop the Dark Side, who is funding her."

He paused, his head in his hands. "I am pretty sure that when you were driving William to the soccer game, she took advantage of the rain and forced you off the road. It was her fault and no one else's." He turned and looked me full in the face.

I let his words sink in. Blythe's fault. *Her* fault, not mine. *Her* fault that my beloved firstborn wasn't with us anymore. And now she was after the rest of my family.

I had never been a fighter. In fact, I was known as the peacemaker among my family and friends—the one who wouldn't confront a waiter if something was wrong with my meal. But this was different. This was *immensely* different.

"I want her arrested!" I screamed.

The taxi driver looked at us through the rear-view mirror and I leaned closer to Sam, teeth clenched. "We have to stop her. She must be held responsible for what she did. She should go to jail for the rest of her life."

Sam nodded and put his lips close to my ear. "I know. I feel like this, too, but we have to have evidence. The best way to right this is to proceed with our plan to meet my French friend and drop off Elizabeth. Then we will have proof—for *this* crime anyway—and we can get additional help to bring her and her sisters in arms to justice."

He glanced at the driver to make sure he couldn't hear us. "Remember, follow my lead and be ready to do whatever I say quickly. We don't always know who is on our side." Sam tapped on the partition between us and the front seat and opened the window. The brown-skinned man glanced at us in his rear-view mirror. "Yes, can I help you?"

"I made a mistake," said Sam. "Our plane is actually going out of Gatwick, not Heathrow. Will you drive us there instead? It will be a shorter drive for you. And you still won't need to give us change."

"No problem. Where are you off to?"

"We are going to Bruges, Belgium on EasyJet. I heard it's one of the most romantic towns in the world."

"Which terminal?"

"That's a good question. I got my mobile pick-pocketed in Stratford. Like an idiot I had it in my back pocket. It has all my info on it. Can I borrow your mobile for just a minute to check my ticket and make a quick phone call? You can add it to my bill."

The driver gestured toward me with his head. "What about *her* phone?"

116

I thought as quickly as I could. "Oh, mine doesn't work in the UK. He didn't pay to upgrade my plan." Sam played along, nodding sheepishly.

The driver passed his mobile back and Sam looked up a flight to Belgium. "North Terminal," he said to the driver. Then he called a number and said, "Hiya, we'll be there soon. Should be in Bruges by 10:00 tonight. We're on our way to the airport now. We'll take a bus or taxi to our hotel. It'll be really late, so we'll meet you tomorrow." He listened for a few seconds and then spoke again. "Yep, looking forward to it, too." Sam deleted the history on the phone and then passed it back to the driver. "Cheers," he said.

Soon we saw signs to Gatwick and the North Terminal. When we arrived, Sam gave the driver more cash. Freya would have to get a lot of money reimbursed for *this* business expense. I made a mental note to ask him for some of the stash in case we were separated again and I needed another breakfast baguette. I wasn't sure how panhandling was regarded in Paris.

I caught up with Sam, who had hurried into the terminal, and without a word, we took the tram to the South Terminal. When we got off the train, our next step was to go through security, but we didn't have tickets. Or so I thought.

"Here," he said, handing me a blue United States passport, "and here's your ticket."

I opened the passport to see the same photo I'd had taken at the post office at home and the correct information. I rolled my eyes at him. "I knew you had a magic bag," I said.

Sam looked confused and I repeated my quip. He nodded. "Yes, the tech gurus at our company *are* magic."

"When did you get this?"

He scanned the immediate environment but continued talking.

"When Freya read your Facebook message, she assumed something was wrong and sent a request to our office for new ones. These are our real replacements, by the way. The company has special privileges. They can expedite even the expedited government branches."

"If they're so good, why can't you just call the office and let them know about Elizabeth and Blythe?"

He sighed. "Remember, I said we are on a need-to-know basis. I do have a contact for paperwork, business expenses, but it's more like an admin service. I'm not sure even they know who they're helping or why. Freya would've made up a plausible story for them."

He glanced around again and nodded towards some empty lounge chairs in the reception area. We were surrounded by passengers who were busy talking, eating snacks, checking out their phones. No one even glanced our way.

We sat down and Sam leaned close to me. "Plan C," he said.

More like plan CC, I thought.

"We aren't going to fly to Paris."

"I thought we were going to Bruges."

"I just said that to throw the driver off in case Blythe tries to get info from him. We're still going to Paris, but we can be traced too easily if we fly. What we need to do here is find a way to change up our looks, but not too much." His eyes panned my face. "Can you change your hair color to blonde? Or wear a scarf? There's a Boots here and some clothes shops."

"You want me to buy some boots?" I asked.

Sam chuckled. "No, Boots is a drugstore. I thought maybe you could get some hair color there."

"I can try, but it will take a couple of hours to color my hair if they even have anything like that at an airport. And why do I have to be blonde? That's like fraternizing with the enemy," I said.

"We definitely don't have a couple of hours. I was thinking more like a couple minutes." Sam stood and beckoned me to follow him through security. My heart beat wildly as we tapped our tickets on the electronic scanner and showed our passports to the airline agent. *What if their computer said we were criminals?*

The woman thanked us for our business and sent us through. We dodged the crowds slowly meandering through the duty-free-shopping megastore sampling perfumes and Scottish whiskey and made for the exit and into the waiting reception.

I held my hand out. "Give me some money and let me look around. Let's meet back here in ten minutes." Sam thrust several hundred-pound notes into my hands, and we went in different directions.

Now, this was something I knew how to do! I could scan the stores and find what I needed in no time. None of the three males in my family enjoyed my love of shopping, so I had learned to do it fast and efficiently. I saw an Accessorize! store, the chain where Sam got his shades and hat in Reading and went inside, all the while scanning for blonde women and bargains.

I bought a blonde wig with a braid you could clip or unclip to make your hair appear longer or shorter. The designer was a genius. Sam had mentioned a scarf, too, but I didn't want to stand out. I was going to Paris, so I needed black, and the British store was just too colorful. There was a Cath Kidston, but that was too floral as well as too colorful. I went to the next shop which was more of a boutique. Voila! A black leather jacket and black cigarette trousers. *Tres chic.* I bought those and a fluffy gray scarf.

I felt a thrilling rush of excitement as if I was on one of those makeover shopping shows where you have a certain amount of money to spend to revamp your wardrobe in an hour. This was the part of the show when the contestants started blubbering and a fashion designer popped out from behind a hidden camera and came to the rescue, but I didn't need rescuing. I was in my element.

I left the boutique and scanned the stores further down, and what did I see—trumpet sound—a Harrods! I walked quickly, swinging my bags, and popped into the ritziest department store in London.

"May I help you?" asked an Asian man dressed in a foppish black suit.

I spoke with authority. "Yes, I'm in a hurry to catch a flight, and I need pair of sunglasses and black boots. Size seven."

"Seven in UK or American?"

"American," I said, disappointed in myself for having forgotten to do my accent and remember that UK sizing was different. The shopping high was clouding my judgment.

The clerk pointed out a knee-high pair of leather boots with low heels. "We have these boots in your size, and they are on sale today."

"Perfect," I said and quickly grabbed a pair of silver Ray Ban aviators to match the scarf.

"Do you need hosiery with that?"

"Yes, please. Socks and undergarments if you have those, too." I looked around. "And quickly, please. I'm in a hurry."

"Someone must have lost their luggage," he said. "I don't have a large selection but…" He walked in mincing steps toward the intimates collection.

I passed him throwing things in his direction. "You start ringing this stuff up," I said. "I'll get the other things." I raced to the back and quickly picked up what I needed. A chocolate brown cashmere sweater that would look gorgeous with my earrings caught my eye. What a great feeling to not have to look at the price tags!

"This is all duty free," Asia said as he rang up my purchases.

"That's great, thank you," I said, stuffing my purchases in the bags I already had. "You can keep the box. I just need the boots," I said.

I raced out of the store with my bags and back to the reception where Sam was waiting. "Did you find anything? I went to Hugo Boss and got some things."

"Yes, I found a couple of things that might work," I said, inwardly thrilled.

"Let's go to the restrooms and change. Put anything you aren't keeping in the bin. Five minutes, and I'll meet you by the water fountain."

I hurried into a stall and put on my new luxury items. I was already feeling quite Parisian. I stuffed the clothes I had borrowed from Freya into the small bin as best I could and put on my new wig in the stall. Next came the Ray Bans. I stepped out of the stall and, after tucking some loose strands of chestnut under the wig, admired the glamorous woman in the mirror. Ooh. Too bad I hadn't picked up a lipstick. I desperately needed a slick of color on my lips.

I went out to meet Sam, and I saw him leaning over the water fountain. He was wearing black jeans tucked into black leather motorcycle boots, a black turtleneck sweater, and a black leather jacket. He had exchanged Arthur's leather bag for a gray nylon rucksack.

I came up behind him and patted him before he could turn around. He jumped a little when he saw me, and then we both started laughing. "Great minds think alike," he said as he put his silver Ray Bans on.

He grabbed my hand and we glammed back out of the airport with our heads held high. Sam flagged down a taxi and gave the driver an address to a car hire nearby. While he went inside, I kept my eyes open for blondes other than myself. The sun was still out and shining, but the air was starting to cool. I zipped up my new leather jacket and fluffed my scarf higher around my neck.

The car park was filled with a variety of small cars and a few SUVs, and I was hoping for the Land Rover when Sam walked out carrying a couple of helmets.

"What? Motorcycles?"

He handed one of the helmets to me. "Marion, you know how to do this. It'll be fun," he said.

"It's been a long time," I said, "a *really* long time."

"It's no big deal. It's like riding a bike. You never forget." He laughed at his own joke.

"We'll see." I had to admit I was kind of excited, but in a scared kind of way. Before the boys were born, Sam and I had rented two bikes for a week and ridden from Ohio to Texas. It was an exhilarating trip. We'd felt young, free, and...hip.

Our hire included black helmets and black bodysuits to wear over our clothes to protect us from the elements and prying eyes.

Sam handed me a Cadbury chocolate bar with hazelnuts.

"Oh. Nuts," I said, and was immediately chagrined.

"That one's mine," Sam said, taking it back and handing me a plain chocolate one. "I know what kind of chocolate my wife likes."

We munched on the bars and practiced hand signals to communicate with each other on the road. Plan ZZ, or whatever we were on now, was to drive to Dover to Le Tunnel and take the train that ferries cars and bikes under the English Channel from England to France.

"Pay attention to my signals," said Sam, "because we'll pull over when I find a good spot. We'll hide your bike and pick it back up later. Hopefully Blythe will think we flew to Belgium, but even if she picks up our trail, she'll be looking for two bikes, not one. You can ride on the back of mine and hold on to me."

"That sounds fun," I said, and meant it.

I made sure my long blonde braid was securely attached, pulled on my helmet, and then pulled the hair back through a hole in the helmet. "How do I look?" I asked Sam.

"Sexy," he said, flirting.

"Ha!" I said, as I slung my leg over the seat, fired up the bike, and got used to the feel of the throttle. I was pleased at how my muscle memory kicked in. Minutes later, I followed Sam out of the car park and onto the motorway.

Sam thought it would take about ninety minutes to reach Dover unless we got stuck in traffic, but I had a feeling he'd chosen the bikes so we could get through any traffic we encountered. We couldn't see any scenery from the motorway, but that was fine with me because I was completely focused on being safe and keeping up with my husband.

At some point, I started noticing signs for Canterbury and remembered reading *The Canterbury Tales* in high school. A group of socio-economically diverse travelers banded together to make a religious pilgrimage from London to Canterbury. To pass the time, each pilgrim had to share a story to entertain the other pilgrims and pass the time. Chaucer had died before he finished writing all the pilgrims' tales.

We were on a sort of pilgrimage, too, and I prayed we would be able to finish our tale so we could entertain Bear and Mom when we got back home. At the thought of Bear, I felt a thud in my stomach. We had to find a way to call or Skype him.

When we neared the Canterbury exit signs, Sam signaled for me to follow him off the modern motorway and into the ancient town.

Thousands had traversed this path over the years and been greeted by the same glorious sight. The Canterbury Cathedral loomed high over the town but, at first, we passed adorable small stone houses with pastel doors, and rode slowly over an arched stone bridge. Sam turned down a side street, and we followed signs to a car park.

"We'll leave your bike here and keep going to Dover on mine." We had to prepay at an automatic ticket kiosk and attach the paid parking ticket to the bike, but a handwritten sign taped to the machine read, "Cash and cards not working. Coins only."

Sam frowned. "What a pain. I don't have any coins."

"We can't leave it without the parking ticket. It might get towed and traced back to you. Then Blythe will be able to figure out where we're going."

"All right, sexy, let's go find some change."

I took off my helmet and tossed my blonde braid just for the fun of it.

We walked down another side street that only had more of the adorable pastel homes, some covered in climbing roses of all colors.

I loved this place. *Could any other country possibly have more beautiful towns and villages than England?*

We quickly reached the pedestrian-only High Street, adorned on both sides with quaint shops and cafes on the bottom floor and one- and two-story apartments above.

Sam gestured toward one of the shops. "There's an ice cream store. Go in there and get us some change," Sam said.

I shook my head. "I'm going to get change in *there*," I said and pointed to a black-and-white timbered inn perched next to a small bubbling stream.

"Go on, then, but hurry."

The Weaver's Inn was a pub now, but the name and "Circa 1500" was painted on its side. I went through the low door and entered another world of timber and stone walls with low beams, old but comfortable looking mismatched chairs and tables, and—of course—a roaring fire in a huge stone fireplace. Patrons were drinking pints, laughing and chatting.

"Are you eating or just having a drink?" asked a huge aproned man with a gap in his front teeth.

I remembered to speak in English this time. "Sorry, I just need to get some change for the car park. The pay machine is rubbish and only takes coins."

"No worries," he said and reached in his apron pocket and pulled out a fistful of pounds. "It's ace to get rid of all this weight I been carrying around. You got a tenner or a score?"

I had no idea what he meant so I held out the twenty-pound note. Apron grabbed it gleefully and handed me two handfuls of coins in return.

"Score!" he said and called out to the bartender. "Mate, I lost twenty pounds already on this new diet I'm on. You only lost a stone. You owe me a fiver."

"Cheers," I said and hurried out whilst the barman argued that Apron had cheated on his diet and said he wasn't paying up.

I held out two fistfuls of coins to Sam. "This is too much," he said. He counted out five pounds worth and said he didn't want to bother with the rest.

"Give it back to me. I know what to do." I crossed the street to where a young teenage boy was playing a guitar and singing melodically. His guitar case was open on the pavement and some coins were inside it. I flung the rest of my money in the case, called out, "Fantastic voice," and ran back across the street.

"Thank you, Madam, thank you," he sang.

"Let's go, Mrs. Philanthropist," said Sam.

As we pulled out of town to continue our pilgrimage, I wrapped my arms tightly around my husband. Our progress to Dover was mercifully uneventful, and we followed the signs, cars and trucks to Le Tunnel. We bought a ticket and joined the queue of vehicles going to the drive-through customs kiosk. From there, we would drive onto Le Shuttle.

As we idled in the queue, Sam opened his rucksack and took out two navy blue Canadian passports and handed one to me. "This is the risky bit of our trip. Let's study up. We're Canadians now and going to France for holiday. If they ask where we are staying or anything else, let me do the talking."

I looked at him with mock naiveté. "So, we're just now getting to the risky bit, eh?"

I studied my new name, birth date, and other details. The woman in the picture had brown eyes and vaguely similar features to me... and bright blonde hair.

Sam leaned over and whispered. "I'm hoping you can keep your helmet on because of the picture. Remember, you're Canadian."

I looked up ahead. "True," I said. "Go, Mr. Canuck, it's our turn next." I said a silent prayer of forgiveness and a plea for help.

Sam passed our fake passports through the window partition and did a reasonably good Canadian accent answering easy questions like how long we would be in France and why were we going. "We're on holiday just for the weekend," was deemed an acceptable answer, and we made it through the English customs and a second time through the French side without having to take our helmets off.

Success! Formidable! *Merci beaucoup.* Today was almost done. Our successful crossing would be a good omen for the next part of our pilgrimage. Make an exciting ride to Paris, get rid of Elizabeth, and let the authorities arrest Blythe while we went back to normal life at home with Bear and Mom. I wanted to ask Sam if he thought *they* were safe, but I'd have to wait until we stopped somewhere. Our hand signals weren't that advanced.

8

Parlez-vous Francais?

The sun was setting as we rode through Calais.

I half expected to see angry refugees chase us and try to steal our motorbike and flee on it to the UK, but the news, as always, was exaggerated, and we made it uneventfully out of the port town.

Sam headed north, and as it got dark, he rode into an adorable preserved medieval French village surrounded by a high stone wall. The streets were narrow, dark, and empty. I assumed the French were eating their quiche and crème brulee and drinking their champagne at home, and I hoped we could soon have some, too. A wooden sign hung in front of a house that read, "Chambre à Louer." I tapped Sam's shoulder and pointed to it. He stopped and put his foot down to brace the bike.

"What does that mean?" he asked.

"Chambre means room, but I'm not sure what the other word means. Maybe it means they have a room available. I can go in and ask." I had been waiting twenty years to practice my college French in an actual French-speaking place. I carefully pulled the helmet off and adjusted my wig and hairpins, wondering if I had permanent brain damage from trying to be Elsa.

"Do you see any of my hair showing?" I asked Sam.

"*Oui, un peu,*" he said, tucking a strand gently under my hairpiece and brushing my cheek with his fingers. "I already feel the romance of France," he said.

I rolled my eyes. "You're so easily distracted from the task at hand. I don't know how you've been a spy," I said.

"I didn't have you around to distract me."

His flattery was working.

I went inside the house and rang a bell at the empty reception desk. An elderly woman attired in a black dress, red scarf, black heels, and red lipstick came from a different room. Her grey hair was cut in a chic bob. The French didn't disappoint.

"*Bonsoir,*" she said, and I imitated her greeting.

"*Parlez-vous Anglais?*" I asked her, chickening out from attempting to ask for a room in French.

"*Oui.* Would you like a room?" she said in a lilting accent.

"*Oui,*" I responded. "Just for tonight for me and my husband."

"Would you like *petit-de-juener*? It is cinq euros per person."

"*Oui. Merci beaucoup,*" I said. I had also been waiting twenty years to try proper French food.

Sam came inside and the proprietor asked us to sign her guest book. We signed our Canadian names, took the old-fashioned brass key, and followed her upstairs to a rustic room. It was plain and delightful. I am prejudiced to like anything the French had to offer.

"I will be downstairs if you need anything. *Au revoir,*" she said, and she shut the door behind her.

I turned to Sam. "I love France. That woman didn't even ask for our credit card or our passports. She only wanted to know if we're eating *petit de jeuner* in the morning."

"I hope you said *oui*. I'm starving. Should we take a shower first or try to call Bear and your mother?"

His tone was almost too casual. "Call Bear," I said, and then paused, a frightening thought appearing around the edges of my mind. "You don't think Blythe would do anything to them, do you? Not if she's over here."

He didn't answer my question. "We'll soon see."

I called the front desk and asked, in a mishmash of English and French, if there was a computer we could borrow. Madame France willingly obliged and Sam and I went downstairs and followed her into a little office behind the front desk. She discreetly left us and closed the door behind her.

Although the walled village looked archaic, the computer had access to the internet and was set up with Skype. Luckily, I remembered to pull my wig off when we saw that Bear was online. I was teary-eyed when my tall, dark, handsome son smiled at us. "Hey, Mom. Hey, Dad. How's the trip going?"

"Great, great," answered Sam, before I could get in a word. "How's orientation?" I remembered that Sam always responded like this when he was on his so-called business trips, and I had never suspected anything.

"Most of my classes will be fine but I think anatomy might kill me," said Bear. "Maybe I don't want to do pre-med after all."

Only a week ago, this school news would have really concerned me. I would have gotten all upset and wanted to convince him to stay the course. Now, I was just thankful he appeared to be okay.

Sam was more encouraging. "Don't let one class discourage you. Try to find a tutor to help you. You take after your mom, which means you're smart. Stick with it." Then he smoothly changed subjects. "Bear, a colleague of mine from work might be near you. I thought she might look you up. Her name is Blythe Marsh—*Ms.* Marsh to you. You met her at Wills'…you know…at his service." It was always hard for the three of us to know which words to use for what happened and we tended to avoid them. Funeral. Died. Passing. Death. Memorial. The words made it so real. My favorite was late. I read it in a book set in Africa, and it seemed not so final. My son is *late.* That's all. Late.

Bear shook his head. "No, I don't remember, and I haven't met anyone who says they know you. I did get a package, though, that was kind of strange. I thought it was from you because it was postmarked from England, but when I opened it, it was an old red flip-phone that I can't get to work. The battery died, and it didn't have a charger. Did you send it to me? I thought it was probably supposed to be a joke, but I don't get it."

Tense, I leaned in to the computer screen. "Where is it?" I asked, in what I hoped was a calm, nonchalant voice like Sam's.

"I'll find it," he said, and we watched him on the computer screen move piles of clothes and books around. Then, we all knew where the phone was—the distinctive old-fashioned phone began ringing. When Bear grabbed it from the floor, we could see that it was exactly like the one Blythe had left for me.

Sam and I both yelled at the same time to tell him not to answer it, but it was too late. There was a slight delay on the video, and we watched as he pushed a button on the screen and said hello. He put his hand over the phone and said to us, "You're acting like it's a bomb or something."

Sam and I looked at each other and I grabbed his arm, but what I really wanted to do was jump through the computer and snatch the phone out of my son's hand. I'm sure Sam was thinking what I was thinking—it might actually *be* a bomb. What was definite was that it was Blythe. She was hunting Bear now.

While time froze for us in France, our son listened to the phone a moment, looked at the phone, then pressed a button to end the call. He came back close to the computer screen and sat back down in front of us. I swallowed hard. "What did she say?"

"Is this a joke?" asked Bear. "You must know who it is, because you said 'she.' She said in a weird computerized voice to listen carefully and do exactly what she says and then no one would get hurt. She said she will call me back in five minutes. What's going on? Is this some kind of hidden camera TV show?"

I wanted to speak, but Sam punched my leg. That was fine, because all I could think to do was to yell for Bear to call nine-one-one, but I didn't think that would help.

Ever calm, Sam said to his son, "Bear, this is very important. Really, really important. This isn't a TV show. This isn't a joke. This is real, and it's possibly dangerous. I want you to get your regular phone, keys, and wallet—nothing else—especially not the red phone. Run to your car and drive to Grandma's house. Don't speed but don't stop for anything or anybody. I think you have five minutes to get to your car before something dangerous happens. Skype us when you get to Grandma's. Now go!"

My husband's voice was so low and clear and authoritative that Bear obeyed him immediately, just like he did when his football coach spoke. "Yes, sir," he said, and leapt to his feet.

We watched as Bear grabbed his keys, wallet, and phone and ran out of his dorm room. He left the red phone on the bed and we heard it ring again. I rocked back and forth, praying to myself.

I looked a Sam. "What will she do to him?"

"She wants to scare us. She is letting us know that if we don't give her what she wants, she can get to Bear." I felt the blood drain from my face and Sam must have seen it.

"She isn't there, Marion. She hasn't had time to fly to America. She's either still in England or following us to France—which we have to assume she's doing. But she probably has an accomplice somewhere there." He paused. "Now we need to call your mom."

"Oh, God, please let her pick up, please let her pick up," I begged as I typed.

My mother was surprisingly good at technology for her age and always liked learning the newest social media platform and getting the latest phone updates. She said she wanted to be a cool grandma, and Wills and Bear had bragged about her to their friends. She was excited to learn how to video chat to see us on our trip and to keep in touch with Bear while he was at school.

I knew I'd received another answered prayer when I heard my mother say, "Marion, is that you?" in a delighted tone of voice. Her face came into focus on my screen and her expression changed. "Where are you? You both look a little disheveled."

My mother considers it her job to continue to improve me. I started to answer, but Sam nudged me hard on the thigh again. I glanced at him, reminding myself to tell him later that we needed to come up with a less painful code for "Don't talk."

"Cheers, Mom!" said Sam. "We're in London, of course, but Marion and I need to talk to you about something important. Are you alone?"

My mother nodded and held up her eleven-year-old silver miniature poodle. "It's just me and Snooky."

"Hi, Snooks," Sam said casually, while I fretted that these social niceties were taking too much time. "I know you've always been curious about my international work experience. It's time to come clean. You're a smart woman, and you've always been appropriately suspicious—"

"I love my daughter and grandsons...son..." she responded.

"Yes, I know. And that's why I owe you the truth."

Mother straightened up and leaned closer to her computer as Sam continued. "I actually work for the military, for a coalition of militaries from several UN countries. It's top secret."

He sounded so credible that I got confused. Was he telling her the truth? I felt him pat my thigh where he'd earlier punched it and I realized what he was doing—he was spinning a story to protect her and to get her to help us without worrying too much.

"This is a matter of multi-national security. My position has been compromised, and our enemies are trying to get to me where it will hurt the most—my family." He paused dramatically. At least this part of his story was the truth.

My dear mother's imagination filled in all the rest. "Is it the communists? The Muslims? ISIS? What can I do to help?"

Sam lowered his voice. "Listen carefully. Do you have an old friend or relative or place you feel safe that Marion and I do not know about?" He emphasized the word *not*.

Mom started to answer, then she paused and said in an equally quiet voice, "Yes, yes, I do as a matter of fact." I couldn't believe it. *How was my family able to keep so many secrets from me?*

"Okay, good," said Sam. "Don't tell us. For both our protection and the United States of America's." He paused. "Mother, Bear will be arriving at your house in about five minutes. Get Snooky, your handbag, and nothing—I mean nothing—else. It must look like you've gone to the grocery store or something normal. To help Bear, Marion, and your country, don't take anything else. Oh, and one more thing. Don't use your credit cards or cell phone. Do you understand? Cash only. And the same for Bear—no phone and no cards. We've talked to him too. He'll do what you say."

"Yes, he will," she said with an authoritative tone. "And, I have a little bit of cash here at the house."

Sam and I both knew she didn't completely trust banks and had cash hidden all over her house. I could imagine her scurrying around collecting it all and feeling quite satisfied that she was prepared for such a day as this.

"Mom, you're the best," continued Sam. "One more thing. Have you gotten any packages? Maybe from England?"

"Yes, as a matter of fact, I have." She got up from her computer desk and walked to the table behind her and picked up a small, unopened package. "It's from England, so I assumed it was a gift from Marion. I was going to make a cup of tea this afternoon to celebrate and open it then."

I thanked God my mother has the ever-rarer characteristic of delayed gratification and said, "Please, Mom, do everything Sam says. Our nation's security rests on it! And don't, don't, don't open the package. Leave it at your house. It's from our enemies."

Sam patted my thigh encouragingly.

"Someone's here!" Mother said. To my relief, Bear appeared behind her on the screen. Snooky barked excitedly, and when Bear came close, the old dog lathered him with wet kisses.

"Hon," I said, "do what your grandma says, and we'll all be fine."

He nodded. "Okay, cool. I did everything you said. When I pulled onto the highway, a lot of cops drove past me with their sirens blaring onto the campus." He smiled. "This is like being in a movie."

"It's *not* a movie, though, Bear," said my mother. "This is real life." She glanced back at the computer screen. "I've been waiting for this news ever since you got married. I always knew Sam was up to something good. I just couldn't put my finger on all the puzzle pieces."

I rolled my eyes, and Sam choked back a laugh. My mother couldn't admit being wrong for anything. She grabbed Bear's arm. "Come on. We're fighting against something big, and we've got some packing to do."

"Don't pack too much, and don't take too long," Sam urged. "The police will probably be on their way to your house. Chances are they've gotten an anonymous tip from one of the bad guys that is meant to distract them—and us—from the real business at hand. Don't believe anything you read or hear in the media over the next couple days. In fact, stay off the internet. You can be tracked. Only answer a call from us. We will keep you updated."

"Yes, sir," Bear said, fist pumping. "I don't mind missing the rest of orientation for this!"

I could hear my mother talking from another room. "Snooky, let's get your leash and your tin of doggie biscuits. We're going on a trip." I bet anything that the biscuit tin contained wads of cash.

Snooky barked in response and I laughed, but something else crossed my mind. "Bear's car," I moaned.

"Right," Sam said.

As Bear leaned down to end the connection, Sam said, "Wait. One more thing before you go. On the way out of town, leave *your* car someplace busy like the mall and then ride in Grandma's car. Grab one of your Grandpa's old not-so-cool hats to cover your head and slouch down low in the seat. Surveillance cameras may be looking for you, and you need to be hidden or disguised."

"Cool, like in *National Treasure*," said Bear.

"More like *Lord of the Rings* when the orcs are coming. In the words of Gandalf, 'Fly you fools!'" I responded.

Bear grinned at us, and the screen went dark.

Sam's stomach made a huge growling sound and mine echoed it.

We both stared at each and then laughed until we gasped for air. It was like a dam of pent up emotions was released.

He wiped tears from his eyes. "Can you imagine your mom running all around the house gathering stashes of money that she probably hid in Snook's doggie toys and beds. And Bear probably got one of your dad's fishing hats—he always made fun of those."

"ISIS. Mom's all excited to fight against ISIS or anybody that's un-American. She's going to tell Bear that she knew this the whole time," I said.

Sam took my hand and tugged. "Let's go back upstairs and try to get some sleep before our breakfast. I hope the word *petit* doesn't mean there won't be a lot of food."

I wanted to stay by the computer longer but I knew we could talk more privately upstairs. I pulled the Elsa wig on my head in case Madame France was still around. "Where do you think she'll go? Where does she have to go that I don't know about?"

Once I'd stepped inside the room, Sam locked the door behind us. "Doesn't she have some family property in Kentucky or Alabama or someplace like that?"

"I don't know about property she has. She has relatives that own hundreds of acres…maybe she's planning to go there. Or she could have some old friend with a place she knows about." I stopped and thought for a moment. "It's funny, but I think I can actually sleep because she seemed really confident. But how will we know that they're all right?"

"Blythe will want us to know because she wants to use them as leverage."

I whimpered. "That's what I'm afraid of."

Sam wrapped his arms around me. "You know what?"

"What?" I mumbled against his leather jacket.

"Your mom is amazing, and so is Bear. I couldn't believe how fast he got to your mom's, or how quickly she got on the plan to leave. They have a little time to get out and going. I think they will be all right."

I wasn't sure if I believed him or not, but I didn't really have a choice. I pulled away from him so I could take off my wig and rub my aching head, wondering if I should shower or just go to bed and hope we could sleep through our hunger. Sam took off his leather jacket and laid it over a striped armchair. With fake seriousness, he said, "You aren't going to believe this."

My heart jumped to my throat. "What? What?"

He pointed to the top of the dresser by the chair. There was a tray with wine and cheese.

I did a jig. "I love the French!" I said. "*Vin, fromage*, et crackers! Sorry, I don't know how to say crackers in French. *Merci beaucoup, Madame France!*"

Sam uncorked the bottle and we sat on the bed and scarfed down our indoor picnic. Sam smiled at me and leaned close for a kiss. "I told you France was romantic," he said.

Surely, this was a good omen. God wouldn't have sent us Freya in the desert if he didn't want us to make it to the Promised Land of Paris, Blythe felt far away, and I had talked to my Bear and mom and they were on their way to a safe place.

On top of that, we had a good plan to finally drop off Elizabeth. The wine was delicious and relaxing and Sam was warm and comforting. Our stomachs sated, we slept a few hours until the sun's rays of hope streamed through a window framed in ruffled white lace.

9

Rendezvous in Paris

When I woke to the sun's rays peeking through the window, I was disoriented. I looked up at the ceiling and saw the dark timbers holding it up and remembered. France, we were in France.

Sam wasn't in bed, but before I could wonder or worry, a key turned in the lock, and he walked in. "*Bonjour!*" he said, holding a silver tray topped with café et pane.

"Bonjour!" I said in return and sat up, fluffing the pillows behind me. Now, *this* was exactly what I imagined our French holiday would be like—sleepy mornings with breakfast in bed and empty wine glasses that reminded of a pleasant evening.

"Voila," said Sam and set the breakfast tray beside me. On it were a white porcelain teapot, two white and blue cups of frothy and steaming café au lait, and a basket covered in a white linen cloth that when unwrapped revealed two golden brown croissants and two golden yellow pain au chocolat. A tiny pot of red fruit preserves, two small white porcelain plates, silver flatware, and a tiny glass vase filled with what looked to me like wildflowers completed the gorgeous arrangement.

Sam sat down on the bed next to me. "Bon appetite!" he said with a smile. I couldn't help but relax at his reassuring attitude. I hoped Mom and Bear were having as good a breakfast in their secret hiding place, and I actually felt no doubt that they were, because no news was good news.

Or was it? I sat up quickly and fumbled around for the TV remote. "We need to check the news to see if there's anything about Bear and Mom." Every channel was in French, though. The news was French or international, but nothing about a grandmother and college student fleeing for their lives in Marion, Ohio, US of A.

Sam looked at me with his usual calm demeanor. "Marion, sit down. Drink your coffee. We won't know anything about them until we get to Paris. Let's have breakfast and get ready to leave as soon as we can."

I turned the news off and sat back down on the bed. The romantic feelings had dissipated, but the coffee was delicious. I slathered some jam on the croissant and took a bite at the same moment Sam took his first bite. Half the layers crumbled all over the duvet, and we both laughed at the mess we made. "It tastes really good, though," I mumbled through a mouthful.

Sam stuffed the rest of his croissant in his mouth and sipped his coffee. "I think Bear understands we are afraid for him, which is good. He'll take hiding seriously. And I know your mother will do a great job of hiding the two of them—if anything, to spite me. Her suspicions were valid about a lot of things, but not everything. I'm one of the good guys," he said, leaning over the bed to kiss me, and then straightening up.

"Ok, get up from this mess you made and put your blonde braid back on. We need to get going. We have to be in Paris and the Tour Eiffel by noon."

I knew from experience that I didn't know when I might get another meal and looked longingly at the vase of flowers and chocolate bread. "Can I put our *pain au chocolat* in your rucksack?" Before he could say anything, I wrapped them up in the white linen cloth and put them in.

I quickly got ready, jammed all the hairpins into the wig, and put the bike helmet over my braid. My head hurt already.

Sam pulled his leather jacket on. "Here's the charade for today, Mar. There are a lot of pickpocket gangs at the Eiffel Tower, and one of them is the contact who will take Elizabeth. It will either be a he—a very dark-skinned Armenian—or a she who looks like a teenaged Romanian."

He donned his helmet. "Possible complications are that we are pickpocketed by a real pickpocketer or Blythe will be there anticipating our next drop attempt. We'll find a place on the way to get some new clothes or a hat." I nodded that I understood.

"And," he continued, "one more possible complication is la police. Because of the recent terrorist attacks in France, there will be a lot of police presence at the Tower, so it may be harder to get pickpocketed than normal. I'll scope it out when we get there."

If I'd been in a cartoon, my eyes would have twirled around in circles. "So, you're saying that we actually *do* want to get pickpocketed, but only by the *right* pickpocketer."

"Oui, that's what I said." He opened the door of our charming chamber and gallantly waved his arm for me to exit in front of him.

Madame France was at her counter, but busy with another couple. She was attired in the same classy black and red ensemble as the night before.

"Merci. Au revoir," I called out as I walked past, protected by my helmet from being recognized by the new couple. Sam put some euros on the counter and waved without looking at the newest patrons.

She smiled and nodded slightly. "Bon voyage!"

Our bike roared to life and we rode slowly through the sleepy village past mothers walking with small children wearing backpacks and old men walking dogs. I tried to remember what day of the week it was, and realized it must be a school day. Every dog seemed pedigreed—no mutts in fabulous France.

We rode through the original town wall, and I looked back longingly at yet another unexplored village. It was even prettier in the morning sunlight and every house and shop front were graced with pots of colorful flowers.

I wrapped my arms tightly around Sam, determined to focus my thoughts on what was going to happen in just a few hours, and not look back—the mental exercise I had developed and strengthened after Wills' death.

The first months were unbelievably painful ones, with tears that seemed unending. Anything could trigger them: a song, a picture, a memory, another boy Wills' age who had some physical similarity. I looked through all our photo albums, my handmade Mother's Day cards, and our home videos, and sobbed. Why didn't I take more pictures? Why didn't I take more videos? If Sam had been home more, he could have taken more. He was better with a camera than me.

I couldn't seem to control my thoughts or emotions and it took a toll on Bear. I realized that I was hurting the boy I still had with me when he started apologizing for laughing at something he'd seen on his phone. I didn't want him to think he couldn't laugh or have fun for the rest of his life!

My friends and colleagues tried to help me too, but it was actually my mother who helped the most. We were all sad when my dad passed away, "went to sleep with his fathers," became late…but he had had cancer. We were all kind of relieved that his physical pain had ended and that Mom could rest from the never-ending and taxing work of caring for him. We had all had a chance to spend time with him, make peace, and tell him goodbye.

But William's life had been snatched from us, and I had had no closure. When I told Mom what happened with Bear, she said that she had been waiting for the right time to talk to me. There was a time for everything, she said, a time to weep and mourn, and a time to move forward to be with the living.

So, I started capturing my thoughts that dwelt on the past and replacing them with something in the present or future. I went back to work part-time at the pediatrician's office. Everyone had been sympathetic and let me take as many days off as I needed, but Mom was right—it was time to get my mind off myself and onto helping the doctors and the children who visited our office. I became the best nurse at giving immunizations—the children seldom saw the needle coming.

Getting Bear ready for college and planning our European adventure had also been instrumental in keeping my mind busy and active in positive ways. My mental capacity to stop a sad, mournful thought and replace it with thankfulness for what I had on that day and that day only got stronger and stronger. I realized my brain, like my arms and legs, was a muscle, and I built it up bit by bit until I could laugh easily again and stop the tears.

It felt like closure, at least with respect to Elizabeth, was coming soon. Hopefully it would happen today at le Tour Eiffel.

We rode on a freeway, so I couldn't see much that looked particularly French-like. As we approached one of the many towns I could see from exits now and again, Sam pulled off and drove us to a store called Monoprix. We parked the bike, walked inside, and I fell in love with France all over again. The store was like a small Target in America. Some clothes, accessories, and beauty items, but also some groceries, wine, and kitchen wares.

I wanted to walk down every aisle, but I focused on the task—to change clothes yet again. I picked a little black dress, oversized sunglasses, a floral scarf, and black flats. Sam bought a different backpack, a gray linen shirt, and a dangling pair of chandelier earrings. He used his bottomless roll of euros to pay for the items and stuffed everything into the British rucksack.

I pointed at the earrings as he packed them. "Are those for you?" I asked innocently. "Is this the way Parisian men dress this spring?"

"Funny girl," he said. "When we get to Paris you'll put on these earrings as a decoy. It's one of the classic pickpocket tricks. A girl will bump you and slide your earring off without you even noticing and drop it. Then while she bends down with you to help you get it, either she reaches around with her other hand or an accomplice grabs something valuable like your mobile or wallet out of your bag or pocket. You think she's all nice and helpful, but later on, you realize you've been robbed." He smiled. "We're going to make it easy to be robbed."

We hurried out and stood by the bike. "Babe," I said, "you make it all seem so easy. How will he or she know that we are the right contacts?"

"We have a code," he said briefly and started to put his helmet on.

"What is it?"

He laid his helmet back down and said very seriously, "I'd tell you, but then I'd have to kill you."

"Sam!"

"I'm just kidding!" he exclaimed, but he still didn't tell me. He put his helmet on and sat on the bike, patting the empty space behind him. I painfully pulled my helmet over my braid again, climbed on, and hugged him from behind. By this time, I had decided that, unlike the adage, blondes *don't* have more fun.

I leaned in close to his helmet. "You wouldn't kill me, would you?" I asked. The question was only half in jest.

He grabbed my hands and pulled me even closer to his body. "I don't think I could live without you."

He started the engine, and we sped off toward gay Paree. As we reached the City of Lights, I noticed the white buildings were all the same height with some modern high rises off in the distance. I recognized the Arc de Triumph from my pre-travel research, and we zoomed under it, following the line of traffic down the Champs-Élysées. I loved it, but I wished we had been strolling down the sidewalk and picking a café to have lunch.

Sam finally pulled off onto a side street, we got off the bike, and he left it in a parking space. All the spaces were small and I was reminded of Steve Martin trying to park his tiny police car in *The Pink Panther*.

"Au revoir," Sam said to the bike, and took my hand. "I got us as close to the Tour Eiffel as I safely can," he said.

We went inside a café with a red awning and happy couples eating lunch and drinking wine at small tables. We asked the waiter, "*Ou sont les toilettes?*" and then proceeded to change our clothes in les toilettes. Sam had instructed me, like before, to bin my old clothes, and I sadly piled my beloved outfit on top. I took off the blonde wig and pulled out the hairpins, handing them to Sam to keep in his backpack. I would need the wig again when we went through passport control.

He handed me the new earrings to put on, and I carefully unscrewed my anniversary earrings and handed them to him. "Bee veery careful with zese," I said, giggling. "Zey are a geeft from someone veery especial to mee."

Sam grinned. "I'll put them in the little outside zip pocket. Then they won't get smooshed with the pain au chocolat."

"Merci beaucoup." He held the pocket open and I dropped them in. After closing the zipper, he took my hand. We walked along the pavement past a café with a green awning and another with a black and gold awning, and when I looked up ahead, I saw our goal, the famous Tour Eiffel. I was frankly more struck by how lovely the park surrounding it was.

Crowds were thronging toward the centerpiece, and we joined in the crush. I could hear all sorts of languages around me including loud and abrasive Americans. Families and couples were relaxing on the green grounds, enjoying a "pique-nique."

I squeezed Sam's hand. "Wouldn't it be nice to come back one day and shop for our baguette et fromage, some strawberries, and champagne, and really enjoy this romantic spot?"

Sam smiled and shrugged. "I think what we're doing is pretty romantic. I mean, look at you. First, you're a hot biker chick in black leather! That speaks romance in my book, and now you're a sophisticated French hottie. Tres chic."

"I feel like a spy Barbie doll with all these costume changes. I didn't know spying could be so much fun. Why have you been holding out on me all these years?"

"Me? I didn't know you would get into it so much and be so

good at it, or I would have taken you into the underground world of spy costumes years ago." Sam squeezed my hand again. "Can you use your British accent as you talk to me, starting now?"

"Sure…I mean, right." I redirected myself with my best attempt at posh.

"Good," he muttered. "We're going to take pictures and selfies and be generic British tourists until the bump. Keep your eyes on me and follow my lead. As you know, sometimes we have to improvise."

I nodded and tried to will the butterflies in my stomach to stop going berserk. This could be fun if it weren't completely scary. Once we dropped off Elizabeth, we could hurry home to Bear and Mom and make sure they were okay. *Focus, Marion,* I said to myself, *you are a British tourist. That's all you have to do.*

Sam took a phone out of his backpack and started taking pictures of the Tower, me in front of the Tower, both of us in front of the Tower. I frowned at him. "Where did you get the phone?"

"At the Monoprix. It doesn't actually work until you put a SIM card in it. It's just for looks."

I nodded. Sam knew how to do things right.

A black-skinned man in a baseball cap and ripped jeans held out his wares to us and asked in English if we wanted a selfie stick or an Eiffel Tower key chain. "Ten euros, good deal. I make you good deal. Ten euros," he said, dangling an armful of gold-colored key chains in our face.

"Make it five euros, five euros, and I'll take a stick," Sam said.

"And a key chain, all for the five euros," I added quickly.

"Ah, smart lady. Pretty lady. Five euros, good deal," and he handed us a selfie stick and a cheaply made but certainly cute key chain and disappeared into the crowd.

"Was that him, did we make the drop?" I asked excitedly. I still wasn't sure exactly what Elizabeth was. Was she information? A code word like a password to a secret account? Or some small item that Sam had somehow kept hidden from me?

I purposefully hadn't looked, asked, or let my mind wonder about it. Instead, I used my mental exercises to stop myself from thinking about what it was, and I believed Sam when he said it was safer for me not to know.

"Well, yes that was an Armenian, but he was a real refugee trying to make a buck—or a euro. He wasn't our guy. Hey, you know that key chain is probably made in China, don't you?"

"I don't care. It was bought in Paris. That's the important part. I'm helping with the refugee crisis," I said, trying not to be disappointed that we were still waiting to be pickpocketed.

Sam pointed to a young American couple. "Ask them if they'll take a picture of us."

When they heard me speak, they said they loved England and asked where I was from. I blurted out "Devon," and hoped they didn't know anyone from there. I wasn't even sure where Devon was—I only knew it was where they made clotted cream for scones.

"We've never been there," the young lady answered. "We've only been to London."

"You should go if you have a chance," I said. "There are cows and sheep and cream, and it's just lovely, really lovely."

Sam interrupted before I could invite them to come to tea. "Could we take your photo in return?"

"Yeah, thanks," the woman said, and they posed while Sam snapped their picture.

He slowly lowered their phone and stared past them. I tried to see what he was looking at, but I just saw masses of people mostly doing what we were doing. I did notice, however, a group of four teenage girls with clipboards. They were interviewing tourists.

Sam handed the phone back to the young man, who looked on his phone at the picture. Then Sam surprised me by asking the man to give him the phone again. "I have an idea. I can take a better picture of you two. Stand back to back and lift your arms up. It will be an interesting perspective picture."

They shrugged their shoulders and the woman said, "Cool, let's do it."

They stood back to back and lifted their arms up, and Sam took their picture again. "It looks like you're holding up the Eiffel Tower," he told them.

When they put their hands down and started walking towards us, I noticed Sam taking pictures beyond them. What was he doing?

Sam muttered to me under his breath. "Keep them distracted," he said.

Without skipping a beat, I turned to the couple and asked about their trip to London, where they lived in the U.S., and what they were doing in Paris. They enjoyed listening to my English accent and answered all my questions. In return, they asked me more about Devon.

"Do you have cows?" asked the man.

"We did, yes, we did have cows," I said trying to think quickly. "We were a small mum and pop operation. We only had a few cows that we milked to make Devon clotted cream. My mum made the cream, and I sold the dear cream pots to local tea shops."

I paused. "But since my father, dear old man, passed away last Christmas, we couldn't bear to see the cows anymore and sold them. It still breaks my heart to think of Daisy being sold, but it was worse to see Daisy lowing and mooing as if asking where my father was."

"Your father died at Christmas? That's terrible," said the sweet girl.

"Yes, that it was. It happened on Christmas morning. My dear old father went out to milk the cows as usual. Cows don't know Christmas is a holiday, do they now? My father didn't come back to the house that morning. So, my husband," I nodded towards Sam and noticed for the first time that he wasn't standing there any longer, "went out to look for him and found him by the cows."

I turned my body in the opposite direction so the couple wouldn't notice Sam was gone. They shifted around and leaned in to hear my story. "He died of a heart attack, but he was doing what he loved best, taking care of the animals."

I looked up to see Sam returning. "So, that's why we got rid of the cows. It's a bad reminder."

The American man was suddenly suspicious of us and turned around. "Where's your husband? He has my phone!"

Sam immediately appeared beside us and handed the Monoprix phone to the young man. "Here you are, mate. Great photos you'll find on there. Quite a laugh. Sorry, but we must carry on," Sam said, taking my hand and propelling me forward.

"Bye!" I called back in the high-pitched voice of the English, and then turned back to Sam. "Where did you go? As soon as that couple sees their phone, they're going to start screaming and call the police."

"That's why we need to duck and hurry. This way," and he steered me through the crowd.

"What did you see? The pickpocket? Or is Blythe here?"

"No, worse. I suspect an imminent terrorist threat."

"What? Terrorists? We need to get out of here!"

"I need to show these pictures to the police. All these people here might get hurt if I don't warn them."

"Sam, this is a distraction. We need to find the Romanian Armenian and drop my earring! We need to go home!"

Sam stopped suddenly and looked at me. I knew he wanted to walk and have me follow, but he purposely paused and spoke slowly and carefully. "Believe me, Marion, I want to make the drop and go home and see Bear and even your mom, but if terrorists are here, this is bigger than us. We have to think of the big picture, of more than just ourselves."

It struck me why Sam could justify hiding his life from me all these years—he was looking at the big picture of stopping bad guys. He'd known I was keeping our family safe and taking care of everything at home. I'd always thought he was selfish, but he had been completely self*less*. "Whatever you say," I told him, and, for the first time, I really meant it.

He nodded. "Thanks for talking to those kids and keeping them distracted. I'm sorry I had to take their phone, but it is for a really good reason. I need to show the cops here. I need to find the decision maker, and I think I know where I can likely find him or her."

He turned away from the swarms of French police wearing their riot gear and carrying what looked to me like machine guns. Les policiers were stationed all around the base of the tower. People were queued to go through a security gate. It seemed like the safest place in the world.

"There are a lot of police out since the terrorist strikes in Paris and Nice, but there do seem to be even more than usual. They must suspect something," said Sam. He turned me around and headed away from the base.

We walked toward a white van parked further away from the main park. "We are in a terrorist war, and just like in all the movies we've watched about war, the general is back with his decision makers off the battlefield while his foot soldiers are closer to the action. I am guessing who I need to find is in this van, but here's the catch. If I expose myself, they will want to hold me for questioning, and that is time I cannot afford." He paused and looked around. "I am going to try to find a way to get the phone to someone in that van without them putting *me* in the van, but I want you to be far from the action. If something bad is going to happen today, I don't want you anywhere near the Eiffel Tower."

He stopped and turned me toward him. "Do you remember that restaurant that we changed clothes in on the way here called Le Café du Vin? Walk that way, and I will meet you out front. Remember, you are the queen of clotted cream, so don't forget your accent." He handed me the backpack. "Oh, and Marion, don't look back. Just walk."

I started walking, trying not to walk too fast or too slow. I wanted to look back, but I was starting to understand that for his safety, my safety, and the safety of thousands of people innocently snapping pictures and licking ice cream cones, I needed to help Sam by not having him worry about me.

I paused in front of a carousel trying to get my bearings. I looked towards my left and thought we had come from that direction. I needed to retrace my steps and go past the café with the black and gold awning, then the one with the green awning, and then I would be at our café, the one with the red awning.

"*Parlez-vous Anglais?*" A curly-haired brunette girl with tanned skin, about fifteen years old, stepped in front of me holding a clipboard. I knew she was too young to be the contact, so I tried to brush her off. "No, no, love, I'm not interested," I said in my best English accent.

"Do you speak English?" she asked and smiled at me.

"Yes, but I'm not interested," I reiterated.

"You don't have to buy anything," she said in very good English with a lovely French accent. "I'm just taking a survey for my school. If I can survey twenty people, I will get an A in my class. I'm almost done. If I can ask you the questions, I will be done for today."

I wanted to help this teenaged gypsy, even if I didn't believe her story about school. She probably did have to do a certain number of surveys for her gypsy boss or whoever was in charge of the pickpocket girls. I told her she could ask me questions as we walked and headed in the direction Sam had sent me. If something was going to explode or a crazy truck driver was going to drive through the Champ de Mars, then I didn't want her or me anywhere close.

"Question one. How many days are you staying in Paris?" she asked.

"Five," I lied, but I wished it was the truth.

"Five," she repeated. "Question two: What is your favorite place to visit in Paris?"

"The Eiffel Tower," I answered, because it was the only place I'd visited in Paris.

"The Eiffel Tower," she repeated. "Question three: What is your favorite food to eat in Paris?"

Suddenly I wondered if one of these questions was the secret code Sam told me about. What if this teenager was really a thirty-year-old in disguise? How could I tell?

"Favorite food?" I hadn't eaten any food in Paris yet. "French fries—or chips—as we say in England."

"French fries," the girl repeated and wrote my answer down without commenting on the chips bit.

About that time, I was pummeled from behind. "Ow!" I exclaimed involuntarily.

"You dropped your earring!" the survey girl squealed as she bent down to pick up, yes, my chandelier earring from the pavement.

These girls were good. I hadn't felt a thing. In fact, I put my hand up to my ear to check that it was actually my earring on the ground, and my ear was bare. Then I froze. *Was this a real gypsy or the contact?*

I took one arm out of my backpack and shifted it around to my chest. The girl remained bent down and I knew I was supposed to lean down to get the earring so she or the person who bumped me would steal from my pack, but what if this was the wrong person? Where was Sam?

I slowly leaned down and moved my hand toward the earring. The pickpocket girl leaned close to me and said in a British accent, "Are you all right?"

"Yes, yes, I'm all right," I answered, even more confused. "Are you?"

She laughed, handed me the earring, and took my hand. She stood up and pulled me up with her. "We'll be fine," she said. "Where's our friend?"

I couldn't help breathing deeply and feeling more relaxed around this girl, but I was jealous. Either the spy agency hired teenagers, or she disguised her age quite remarkably.

Before we could say or do anything else, we both jumped at the sound of fireworks, and the Eiffel Tower lit up with sparkly lights. The entire crowd of tourists oohed at the same time, and I looked up at the sight and gasped in delight.

The girl grabbed me and yelled, "We've got to run! The Tower only lights up at night. They've set off the fireworks as a distraction. Follow me!"

Gypsy Girl took off towards the right in the opposite direction from where I was supposed to meet Sam. She looked back at me and beckoned for me to follow. I started her way, then stopped. She was probably right that the lights were a distraction, but I needed to trust Sam and stick to the plan.

Gypsy Girl looked back. "Follow me!" she yelled. "I'll take you to Sam!" I saw the flash of something silver and black in her hand—a small gun. "Follow me," she yelled again and waved it in my direction.

Instead, I reversed course and ran away from the girl and, as the Tower sparkled and crackled and the crowd cheered, I heard another sound behind me—the sound of a gunshot. It seemed closer to the Tower than where the girl had last been, but I put Sam's words into practice once again, and putting my head down, ran in the direction of the café.

10

Fireworks and Gypsies

"Café du Vin, Café du Vin," I muttered over and over to keep focused. People were running and screaming in all directions, so it was hard to get my bearings, but I thought I was moving in the right direction.

My heart raced and my side ached, and I fully expected to feel a bullet in my back. I was still clutching Sam's rucksack and stopped to slip my arms through the straps. With it on my back, I could run faster. Maybe, too, it would protect me a little more.

A little girl was lying on the pavement below me. The crowds were jumping over her to keep from tripping and I knew that eventually someone was going to fall on her. You always hear that more people die during a riot from falling and getting crushed than from gunshots.

Kneeling down beside her, I tried to buffer her body with mine. It was dangerous down low, but I knew instinctively that Gypsy Girl would have a harder time getting a clear shot at me.

La petite fille was crying and calling in French, and while I couldn't understand her every word, I did recognize the universal word for "Mama." Her hands and knees were scraped and bloody, and my nursing and mothering instincts kicked in.

"*Bonjour, je m'appelle Marion*," I told her. I held my hands out slowly and smiled so she could see I was friendly and moved to lift her up. People pushed all around us. Petite Fille let me help her stand up, and I said, "Ooh, la la," in a sympathetic voice. She babbled again in the loveliest little voice, but she spoke way too fast for my twenty-year-old French to catch up. I picked her up and slung her legs around my waist.

Petite Fille was probably five or six years old and light enough for me to carry a short while. She looked over my shoulder and said, still with a sniffle, "La Tour Eiffel est belle!"

I glanced back and could see the fireworks were still going and the base was covered in smoke. I had been running uphill in the Champ de Mars, and my vantage point now enabled me to better see the chaos below.

"Oui, c'est belle!" I said into her ear, hoping she would stay calm until I found help.

By the Tower's base, French police and military were shouting into megaphones, and I could see they had their mob shields lifted and were moving the crowds away. Looking up ahead, I noticed more police and soldiers shouting and lifting their shields and walking in my direction. They were going to barricade us in!

I heard sirens wail from white and red ambulances pulling up behind the police. Clasping la Petite Fille close to me, I pushed towards one of the ambulances. "*Excusez-moi, excusez moi! Aidez moi, aidez moi! Elle est hurt!*" I called out in mostly French.

People saw the blood on the girl's hands and her tears and parted for me to squeeze through. As the police crushed everyone in one direction, I managed to reach an ambulance and told the paramedic dressed in white, "*Excusez-moi, aidez-moi! Parlez-vous Anglais?* Elle est hurt. Elle est lost from her Mama." I transferred the girl into the paramedic's arms, and told the girl in English, "You will be okay. He will take care of you. Bye, bye, au revoir."

She stared at me with her big brown eyes, and the paramedic spoke French to me, but as with the little girl, it was too fast for me to understand. "*Je ne sais pas. Merci, au revoir,*" I kept repeating while I waved good-bye to Petite Fille and rushed out of the soon-to-be-cordoned-off area. Most of the crowd was now blocked inside the police ring, so I had a little more space to run.

I felt guilty for leaving Petite Fille, but she hadn't been hurt very badly, and I was sure the paramedic would be able to find her mother. "*Merci beaucoup, Petite Fille,*" I whispered. "Thank you for helping me get out of there. I pray you find your mother very soon."

When I reached the boulevard Sam and I had walked along earlier, I started asking passersby, "*Ou est Café du Vin, sil vous plait?*" Most people shrugged and continued running away from the Champ de Mars, but one elderly man pointed in the direction I was already walking.

My mind raced. *What if I got to the café, and Sam wasn't there?* I needed a plan. I could change back into my blonde wig and wait a while. If he didn't return, I guessed I could use my return ticket to fly back to London. And then do what? If Sam didn't meet me at the café quickly, should I go to the American Embassy? *Aidez-moi, s'il vous plait.*

This whole thing was just getting bigger and bigger. Bear and Mom were in trouble. Terrorists were at the Eiffel Tower. I was separated from Sam. Gypsy Girl hadn't gotten Elizabeth from Sam, and she may have been planning to shoot at me. *C'etait trop.* It was too much.

I spotted a café with a black and gold awning ahead on my left. The red awning of the Café du Vin was two doors down, but there were no longer happy couples sipping wine or café lattes out front. Sirens were still screaming in the background, and everyone seemed to go into hiding. I pushed the door open and disappeared inside.

There stood Sam. I shouted his name and ran to him.

"Marion!" he said, picking me up and swinging me around. I felt immediate relief. Sam was back in charge, and I wouldn't have to figure out which bad plan to follow next.

"What happened?" I said once I'd gotten my breath.

"You first. Are you all right?" he asked, holding my upper arms and looking me up and down.

"Yes, but are we safe here?" I asked. "There's a girl who did the earring trick to me, and then when the fireworks went off, she told me to go with her to find you. I didn't trust her and came back to here. She held out a gun, Sam, and pointed it at me."

He rubbed my arms lightly. "It was a gypsy girl and not a man?"

The café door opened and a bell hanging overhead cheerily announced a customer. "That's her! She's got a gun!" I yelled as the curly haired Gypsy Girl closed the door behind her.

Sam kept his arm protectively around me and looked the girl up and down. She extended her hand to him.

"Sorry, about that," she said, looking at me. "I didn't mean to scare you. I was trying to make sure that you were the right person. I expected to meet Sam and I saw you together at first, but then he seemed to disappear."

Sam held his hand out towards her and said, "Gun?"

"It's in my back pocket under my jacket."

Sam nodded and I was confused. *Was asking about the gun the signal?* That didn't seem like a good idea.

"It's okay," he said to me. "She's one of us." He waved us over to a little table in the back of the restaurant. We all sat down, and Gypsy Girl held her hand out to shake mine. I ignored the girl's friendly overture. "She pointed a gun at me."

The girl withdrew her hand. "I was actually pointing the gun at a person behind you. You were being followed."

"Am I supposed to believe that?" I argued. "How do we know you're not the one doing the following?"

"I saw you both talking to the American couple, and I was preparing to approach you and signal for the exchange, but Sam disappeared. I wasn't sure if you would know what to do, so I decided to follow you once the lights went off at the Tower." She nodded at Sam, a realization dawning on her.

"That was *you*, wasn't it? Pretty incredible."

Sam interrupted her. "Go on," he said in a low voice, "we've got to decide our next step quickly."

"I followed her into the crowd and made the connection, but when she took off running, I had to chase her. I couldn't lose both of you. It would have been better for me to stay with her and find you, Sam. I saw a face in the crowd that I noticed from one of our target practices, and the target was heading towards your wife. That's when I took out my gun and showed it to the target. I was prepared to shoot if I had a clear shot, but it would've been hard in that crush of chaos."

Gypsy Girl no longer sounded like a teenager—her voice had taken on the staccato clip of a military officer reporting for duty. "I lost sight of her," she said, gesturing at me, "but then picked her up again carrying a small child towards the emergency vehicles." She paused to look at me. Sam raised his eyebrows at me and I shrugged.

"A little girl fell down in the crowd and was crying for her mom in French. I picked her up and took her over to an ambulance."

Gypsy Girl nodded. "What she did was brilliant. By utilizing the child as a distraction, she managed to exit the cordoned-off area while the police were closing the perimeter."

I smiled at the compliment. I was genuinely trying to help Petite Fille, and she'd ended up helping me, too. Good deeds are like that.

The young woman finished her story. "I was able to slip through the barricade myself and followed her here."

I looked around the empty café and then back at Sam. "What happened to you? And what are we going to do now?"

"I managed to reach one of the police vans and show them the pictures of what I saw at the Eiffel Tower. I suggested they set off the fireworks to distract the terrorists and get the crowds moving. As I thought, they wanted to keep me for questioning, but while they were talking amongst themselves, I ducked away."

He glanced outside. "They obviously took my advice. I would imagine they locked down the area to find the suspects—and maybe me, too. Hopefully another tragedy was thwarted. The whole of Paris is going to be locked down soon, and our gypsy friend will need to get back to home base."

Sam took the backpack out of my lap and slid it across the table to his colleague. "You'll find what you need in there," he said.

I was confused. "What about—"

"I'm sure she's hungry after her long day in the park," he said.

I figured he had hidden Elizabeth in the pain au chocolat. He must have been carrying whatever it was around the whole time.

"Yes, I am hungry," Gypsy Girl said, picking up the bag, and reaching behind her. "But the thing is, sir, I need to take you to home base *with* me."

She pulled the gun from her back pocket and pointed it at Sam. "You are the one who stole this item, and you are the one who is killing off all the contacts. I am under orders to bring you in alive with the item."

She waved her gun at us, and Sam raised both his hands in the air. I raised mine, too. "Your wife, however, does not have the same contract. I was told that if she got in the way of a peaceful arrest, it is permissible to dispose of her."

"What?" I said, with tears welling up in my eyes. "Me? I haven't done anything wrong! Neither has Sam."

"Keep your hands up, both of you, and walk toward the kitchen. We will exit through the back door."

Gypsy Girl waved us along in front of her. Sam turned and walked towards the swinging doors that separated the café from the kitchen and Gypsy Girl kept talking. "Though I'd never met Sam, he has an incredible reputation with the agency. I wasn't positive he had gone rogue. When I was contacted to meet him to receive the drop, I wanted to check his story out for myself. You too are quite the happy married couple."

I turned around to look at her, but she waved the gun at me to turn back. "Today I witnessed Sam saving thousands of people from a possible act of terrorism when he really didn't have time to stop and help. I witnessed Mrs. Sam help a little girl when she really didn't have time to stop and help. I want to take you both in, and I'll share what I witnessed and give my opinion on the matter. In exchange, I need you both to go quietly and not give me any trouble."

Although I was surprised, that was fine with me. I didn't want either of us to be killed, and being taken in to home base, whatever that was, seemed like a great idea.

Then, just as Sam pushed on the swinging door, we heard a loud explosion. We all grabbed our heads and ducked as two men in chef hats and aprons ran out from the back of the kitchen. Pushing past us, they yelled at each other in French, "*Vous verrouillez la porte!*"

"They are saying 'Lock the door, lock the door,'" I whispered.

"We've got to get out. Come on," said Sam.

Gypsy Girl nudged first me and then Sam in the back with the gun. "Go out the back exit," she hissed. "I've got to take care of those men. I don't know how much they heard."

The chefs locked the door and began pushing tables and chairs against it. "They don't speak English," I said. "They wouldn't have told us in French to lock the door if they spoke English."

"*Excusez-moi*," I said to the men, pointing to the kitchen. "*Nous devons partir.*"

"*Vite, vite!*" one of the men replied, and not even noticing the gun, he shoved us through the swinging doors and pointed to a door on the back wall of the kitchen.

"I'll leave them," Gypsy Girl said, "but don't make any sudden moves or trouble. The wife goes first if there are any problems."

My heart started pounding through my chest and I thought I might black out. We were surrounded by terrorists outside and crazy work colleagues inside.

Sam slowly opened the back door. Warm sunshine poured over us, and we squinted after being in the dark café. Seeing daylight made me feel a little better, and we all walked outside into a back alley behind the main boulevard. Shouts and sirens wailed around the corner. "We have tickets to Belgium," said Sam to the girl or woman or whatever she was. "We can go to home base via Bruges."

"All right. Let's see if we can get a taxi and get to the airport," she answered. We headed back towards the main boulevard, and as we neared the corner of the building, a group of French police hurried by us.

"Wait!" I yelled at Sam. Before I could explain, one of the police, a blonde woman, stopped suddenly, turned towards us, and shot at Gypsy Girl, who crumpled to the ground. Sam leaned over her, grabbed the backpack, and yelled, "*Vite!*"

As the police knelt down by the gypsy, Sam and I ran back down the alley and around the corner. Again, I had the horrible expectation of a bullet searing through my vulnerable back, but Sam was behind me, steering me with his voice. "Go left! Around that man. Right! Right! Down this street!"

Somehow, Sam got us back to where we had left the motorcycle. We jumped on and sped off, me holding onto him as tightly as possible. We hadn't taken the time to pull on our helmets, but I was too scared of stopping or slowing down to bother Sam with safety. I felt like we were in one of those car chase scenes in a movie—which I usually didn't like very much—but today we needed to get out of the City of Dark as soon as possible. Our contact was dead or wounded and Sam's bosses apparently didn't mind if I got killed.

What kind of organization did Sam owe his allegiance to? Was he in the British mafia, if there was such a thing?

I wrapped my arms around him and ducked my head behind his back. At the speeds we were going, I didn't know how he could bear his face being unprotected. My teeth were chattering and my whole body was shaking. Finally, Sam began slowing down, and I lifted my head to see where we were. Charles de Gaulle Airport.

"What are we doing?"

He pulled my blond wig and earrings out of the backpack and handed them to me. "Do you remember your Canadian info?" Then he handed me my fake passport. "Here, review this and make sure you have it memorized. We're flying back to London."

I struggled to pull the too-tight wig back on my head and

leaned over the bike's side mirror to check for stray hairs. I pulled off the chandelier earrings and started screwing on my brown gems.

Sam continued to talk. "Security will be tight at the airport and may take a while, but it's our best bet at this point. Memorize everything and no more French."

"So, we're going back to London? Not Belgium? Or home?" I pushed the pins into my head and winced. I couldn't wait to be done with this disguise.

"Home base is in London. I'm going to turn myself in. I don't know who to believe or trust, but I can't put you through this anymore. I've got to go into headquarters. It means I will be exposing myself, because even headquarters doesn't know exactly who their agents are. I'll find you a secure location to stay while I'm there."

I had a million questions again, like did he think Gypsy Girl was dead? What was the explosion? Did he think I could make it through security? I looked up at him, and although he was haggard looking and obviously tired, he put his arm around me and tried to smile. My heart melted, and I said, "You stopped terrorists! That's amazing!"

He shrugged. "I just let the police know what was happening. It was up to them to do something about it. I hoped it worked." He stopped and thought for a moment. "I have a feeling that second explosion was controlled by the police to get the crowds away and the terrorists distracted." Then he looked down at me and put his arm around me. "Thanks, Mar. I'm really sorry. This has really gotten out of hand. All I want to do is make sure you and Bear are safe."

"And Mom," I said.

"Definitely, Mom," he said.

We headed into the airport. "We should buy a suitcase or at least another backpack," I said, "and some liquids, maybe duty free. You know, it would be odd for a couple from Canada to only have one backpack and nothing else." I was glad to have something practical to do like shop to take my mind off everything.

"That's good, Marion, good thinking," he said and took my hand. "Why do you have to turn yourself in? You're not the bad guy."

"In my seventeen years of working for this organization, I've never gone into the office, so to speak. Our business depends on anonymity, and I only know my assignment and my current team, or in the case of Blythe, my partner for assignments. The policy is for our protection and that of our clients."

We stopped in a shop that carried suitcases. I picked a small black one, and Sam paid for it. There was an airline-approved bag of French lotions, body wash and shampoo, and I got one of those, too.

"So, you never went to your office Christmas party like you told me you were doing every year?"

I could tell Sam was frustrated with me. "Marion, I've explained this. No lies now, but when I told you things before, it was for your protection...and mine. Pre-Christmas is a busy time in my business, so I was always on a case. Remember a few years ago when you planned that Caribbean cruise for our family Christmas present?"

I nodded. How could I forget? It was one of my top ten most disappointing life events, and my mom couldn't stop speculating that Sam was having an affair. He'd told me his boss's boss's boss was coming in for the office Christmas party, that they never had enough funds to include spouses, and he had to be there. "I was really looking forward to going on the cruise and being with everyone," he said, "but then a really important, life threatening situation happened in the Middle East, and I had to go. It was important."

From his tone of voice, I realized that even though he said the word "important," it was if he no longer believed it himself. He was starting to doubt himself and we couldn't afford for that to happen. To get out of this situation required that all his confidence and bravado and wits remained intact.

"Sam, forget about it. That's all done. We all got the Noro virus anyway. You didn't miss out on anything." I wrapped my arm around his back and squeezed him. "Let's talk about what's next."

He squeezed me back and smiled. I swooned—my husband is still indescribably handsome when he smiles.

"Yes, ma'am," he said. "Okay. So, I'm going to headquarters, which is at the Shard. I'm going to turn myself in, because I don't know what Blythe may have said about me. I'll put myself in their hands as a loyal employee, hand over Elizabeth, and ask for protection for all of us—including Mom, of course."

"Are you worried about this?" I asked, still not understanding why we hadn't done this in the very beginning.

"You heard what the woman in Paris said. It's what I've been afraid of. Blythe lied to them, too, and they believe her. They won't know which one of us to believe."

He stopped and looked at me. "Mostly though, it means I lose my job. We can only go in when we are ready to end our careers. It's a death sentence."

We arrived at the security queue and I screamed a whisper into Sam's shoulder. "What? A death sentence? You don't mean literally, do you?"

"No, not literally. Career wise."

He grew quiet, thinking. "Maybe it's time for a new job anyway. I can be a soccer dad and you can be a full-time nurse."

"Sure, that's fine. Let's just get to the Shard and get this done."

Sam walked us to the ticket counter and asked to change our flights.

"We really did have tickets to Belgium?" I asked.

"Yes, that's what the tickets that Freya left in the backpack are for, but I always meant to reroute us in case she'd been compromised."

I hated to be reminded of my best college friend's betrayal. Maybe she wasn't on Blythe's side, but she had perpetuated the dishonesty between me and Sam. I know she would say the same as Sam—that the secrets and lies were for our protection—but had the end really justified the means? I would have to ponder that philosophical question when I had more free time once we'd turned Elizabeth in and Sam had been fired.

The French woman at the ticket counter looked stunning in her navy jacket with brass buttons and a crisp white shirt. A colorful scarf was knotted elegantly around her neck, and her brunette hair was in an updo that showed off her red lipstick. *How did these French ladies pull off the sophistication?* When I got home, I would definitely reassess my wardrobe and throw out all my "mom clothes." After all of this, Sam owed me a major shopping trip.

Madame Air France didn't radiate warmth and help as she pursed her lips and made a clicking sound of annoyance at doing her job. She came through with two tickets to London Heathrow, though, and even found us two seats together.

"You are veery lucky today. I have found you thee last two seats on the plane to London. I will have to charge your credeet card with a change fee, but it is your lucky day," she said, handing us boarding passes with our Canadian names.

"Merci beaucoup," Sam told her. "Oui, we are a very lucky couple." I rolled my eyes and couldn't help snickering a little.

We walked away towards security. I was wheeling my new suitcase with the backpack stuffed inside it. "We are veery lucky," Sam repeated only to me.

"I think the word is *un*lucky."

"Marion, you helped that little girl, and by keeping that American couple distracted, you helped me use their camera and get pictures to the police to hopefully stop something really bad from happening. We were veery lucky to have a bottle of wine last night in our romantic chalet and see Bear and Mom. I am veery lucky to have you with me."

"Well, you certainly know how to flip a situation and see the bright side. But you're right. We *are* veery lucky." I looked at him flirtatiously and tried to change the subject. "I was thinking that when we get home, I could do some shopping to incorporate more Frenchness into my wardrobe."

That made Sam laugh. "Oui, that will make me veery lucky."

We went through security with no problems and made our way to customs. The French passport control would look at us and our passport photos and decide our fate. I paused and asked the question I'd been meaning to ask since we'd first arrived in Dover. "What happens if I get caught with a fake passport?"

He walked toward the customs officer with our passports in hand and called over his shoulder. "You go to jail for a really long time."

11

Keep Calm and Carry On

We settled into our seats on the Air France flight and I exclaimed under my breath. "We did it! I did it!"

I couldn't help smugly rejoicing that we made it through with our passports not once but twice—coming into and out of the country. Then I worried about all the bad people that could do that, too.

Surely, though, Sam's company had some kind of government authority to change passports and use different credit cards. Once he'd turned himself in and we were back home, I would make him tell me exactly what kind of company he'd been working for all this time.

"You're definitely getting the hang of it," Sam said laughing. "Don't jinx us, though. We've got a two-hour flight to Heathrow. We should take advantage of all the free food and wine they give us on the flight, because, as you know, we don't always know when our next meal may be. From the airport, we'll take the Heathrow Express to Paddington Station. We'll find a place to stay for the night. In the morning we'll take the tube to St Paul's, walk across the

Millennium Bridge to the South Bank, and from there to the Shard. It will be your first time seeing St Paul's, the Globe Theatre, the Old City of London. You're going to love it."

As had become normal for me the last few days, I had felt an emotional rush of excitement about what I was finally getting to see and do followed by a plummet when I realized I wanted nothing more than to get home safely. At the moment, though, excitement was winning. Surely, making it through customs again was a good sign. After all, Madame Air France had said how lucky we were.

Sam had rescued no telling how many people in Paris, which I hoped meant it was our turn in the circle of life to get through this last part of our adventure safe and sound. I was convinced that Sam needed a career change, so if turning himself in was the catalyst, so much the better.

We sipped our vin rouge, nibbled our brie and cranberry croissants, and finished off our lunch with un biscuit au chocolat. Even the airplane food in France was elegant, I thought. Sam's eyes were drooping, so I squelched the remaining questions I wanted to ask him. Like what would happen if his mysterious bosses didn't believe him?

As we began our descent into London, the pilot told us to look out of the window on our right side. I gasped in delight at the city of London sprawled out below us. I could see the curving Thames River, the bridges crossing it, the London Eye. A tall building appeared in the distance. Was that the Shard looming over all?

Sam woke up, looked over me out the window, and patted my leg. "You're going to love it, Marion. London is fantastic." He filled me in with the next need-to-know details for our foray into the two-thousand-year-old city. "Once we get through British customs, we can't use those passports or the credit card anymore. Blythe will have flagged them by now and will be watching for us."

171

"You mean they could stop us at customs?" I asked.

"I doubt she's been able to infiltrate customs yet, but we will assume she knows we are arriving in London rather than Belgium. She may even think I'm turning myself in, so we have to be careful. I'll tell you what to do as we go along, so just keep in tune with me. Like you've been doing already. You've been fabulous."

I didn't know what he meant by "infiltrate customs," but I really didn't care. "What about my wig? Do I need to keep wearing it?" I rubbed my head which was numb from the tightness. It couldn't be good for my brain.

"Once we get into the airport, you can drop Elsa in the loo. We'll get rid of the suitcase once we're at Paddington. If we abandon it in the airport, we could cause a bomb scare. We want to look like two Americans—no, forget that. Let's be a British couple for the next bit. Got it? Canadian through customs, then British."

"Got it, mate," I said.

Nothing dramatic happened at customs and we bought two train tickets to Paddington with Sam's remaining pound notes. We were now out of cash and had no credit cards, but I assumed Sam had a plan. I went into the ladies' room and gratefully stuck my wig at the bottom of a bin and covered it with tissue. I rubbed my head and hoped there wasn't any permanent damage.

We zipped into Paddington Station on the Heathrow Express with no problems. As we got off the train, I saw a little bronze statue of Paddington Bear. The sight brought back happy memories of reading the books and watching the videos with Wills and Bear.

In fact, Paddington had been one of the reasons we'd given Bear his nickname. He was snuggly and loved hearing me read the books. Wills tried to tease him over it all, but Andrew liked it and the name had stuck. As I walked through the station beside Sam, I thought about our boys. They'd had good childhoods and I needed to remember that. Things aren't always as they seem.

"We're just like Paddington Bear," I said. "We're on an adventure in England, and we keep getting into scrapes even though we have the best of intentions."

Sam looked confused, so I pointed at the statue.

"Got it," he said, laughing. "Paddington."

The station, which seemed made entirely out of steel with windows soaring in an arch overhead, was bustling with passengers getting off and on trains. It was much grander than the other train stations we'd been to in England.

Sam glanced around. "All right, let's ditch the suitcase. We can't leave it in the station for the same reason we couldn't leave it in the airport." The sky above us was overcast and gray, and the air was chillier than it had been in Paris. I saw a bird fly overhead and out an entrance. "I have an idea. Follow the bird," I said and started rolling the suitcase towards the entrance.

It was impossible to walk in a straight line as people zigzagged all around me, walking purposefully to their destinations. A lovely British woman's voice sounded on the loudspeakers announcing arrivals and departures and platforms. Even the mundane sounded nice with an English accent.

We walked outside right into the smoking area. "I think the hospital where Prince George and Princess Charlotte and Prince Louis were born is right around here," I said excitedly.

"We don't have time to visit princes today. What was your big idea?" Sam muttered.

I pointed to an older man shuffling along with a cane and inspecting a bin. "*He* is," I said and wheeled the case over to him.

"Excuse me, I'm done with this," I said, and I leaned over to unzip it. Sam had already taken out the backpack, and I wanted the man to see we didn't have a bomb or anything bad in it. "It's empty now, and we don't need it any longer. Do you know if someone could use it?"

The man looked at me and Sam, then down at the suitcase. "You say it's empty, eh. Maybe I do."

I handed the elderly man the handle, and waved good-bye. "God bless you, Madam," he said. Yes, that was what I was hoping for—God's blessing on the next hour.

Sam shook his head. "You and your homeless friends," he said. He followed the street parallel to the station, which was teeming with workers heading home or to the pubs after work. We reached a picturesque waterway he said was called Little Venice.

Familiar narrow boats lined the canal and I thought of Captain Jack and the Tea Time and hoped he and his wife were doing well. Sam walked to a boat laden and strewn with a plethora of potted plants. The front door had a posted sign stating it was a Book Boat, but a barrier rope crossed the doorway and the door appeared to be locked up.

Ignoring the signs of closure, Sam walked up to the door, knocked, and called out, "Do you have anything good to read?"

By this point, I thought this was probably a signal or code to Sam's colleagues, but it seemed simplistic. Wouldn't ordinary people perhaps ask this question?

"I have a second edition of a C.S Lewis novel," I heard a voice answer from inside the closed-up boat.

"I have a first edition," Sam replied.

"Well, come in for a cup of tea, and let's discuss it," said the voice from inside.

Sam nodded and smiled at me, and we climbed over the rope and went inside the Book Boat. It was dimly lit, but I could see an interior stacked with rows and shelves of books. A white-haired gentleman waved his walking stick at us and pointed to a low sofa. "Can I get you a cup of tea or water or maybe a beer?"

We sank down and dust puffed up around us. Who *was* this man, and why was he so obviously deferential to Sam? Before I could even ask a question, Sam answered.

"Water is fine. We've had a long day, and some light reading before bedtime would be perfect."

Mr. Books nodded and brought us two glasses of water, and a cozy, if slightly grubby, blanket. Sam nodded back an apparent thanks, clinked my water glass with his, and covered us both with the blanket. Our butler of sorts slid away, turning off lamps, and before I could ask anything, Sam was asleep half sitting up. I took his lead, adjusted my position on the soft sofa, and settled in for a nap.

We awoke with the morning sun streaming in through maroon colored curtains. Mr. Books seemed to be waiting for us as he brought a tray of tea, buttered toast and raspberry jam before we could even sit up. I asked for a loo, and he waved his stick towards the back of the boat. Sam was finishing his breakfast when I returned.

"It's time to go. Are you all right?"

"I'm all right," I said. We'd had a good night's sleep on the Book Boat. I knew I should want to know who had taken care of us during the night, but I was merely grateful Sam knew such an unquestioning gentleman.

Sam nudged me out the door, and I thanked our bookish butler as we crossed the threshold and headed back towards Paddington Station. I followed Sam inside.

"The tube is downstairs," he said. "We'll take it underground across London to the river." We followed the crowd going down the stairs all queued in orderly fashion to stand on the right side of the escalator while the walkers moved quickly down the left side. In France, the escalators had been a jumble. We were back on the island of order and manners.

I could see the turnstiles ahead of us where quiet Londoners quickly tapped cards or slid paper tickets to get through the barriers to the tube. It was darker downstairs, and the hall was lit with fluorescent lights. There were a few shops selling snacks, London souvenirs, and reading material. "Do we have to pay to ride the tube?"

"Let's look in the magic backpack and see if there's anything in here," he answered.

He rummaged through it and pulled out two blue cards. "These are oyster cards, and they will either be innocuous and we'll ride the underground and get to St Paul's in twenty-five minutes, or they're being tracked and as soon as we tap in, Blythe will know where we are."

"Let's assume the worst since that seems to be what usually happens to us. Maybe we can trade them with someone else?" I asked.

"Good idea. As we approach the ticket barrier, you create a diversion, and I'll trade cards."

"That wasn't what I meant! I don't know how to create a diversion!" The honeymoon phase of making it through customs, ditching my wig, seeing the Paddington Bear statue, and helping a homeless man was over. Now it was time for a stress-induced adrenaline rush.

Sam strode purposefully toward a group of German tourists, which I was able to deduce from their khaki hiking trousers, sturdy walking sandals, and Jack Wolfskin backpacks. Plus the fact they were speaking to each other in German.

The group had their oyster cards in hand to go through the ticket barrier. I did a little skip to catch up with Sam, and he gave me a meaningful nod. I did the first thing that came to my mind, and purposefully skipped again, stumbled forward and fell down, knocking down one of the German's suitcase as I went. A German man leaned down and picked up his suitcase first, then he asked me in his accented English if I was all right.

I held my hand up to him, smiled, and asked in an English accent, "Oh, sorry, can you please help me up? I must have slipped on some water back there, and my ankle hurts."

He hesitated, then leaned over, took my hand, and pulled me to my feet. Sam took the German's other hand in a handshake and started shaking it heartily. "Sorry to bother you, mate. Thank you ever so much for helping my wife. She can be quite clumsy."

I thought Sam's fake accent sounded cheesy, but I just smiled at the man and muttered, "Clumsy me."

"How is your ankle?" asked Sam, giving me a thumbs up.

"All better now, thank you." I nodded at the German man. "Sorry again. Goodbye."

Sam handed me an oyster card, we tapped in, and made our way through a labyrinth of tunnels and escalators that seemed to be taking us to the bowels of the earth. "Why doesn't this collapse under the weight of the entire city?" I asked.

"It's been here for over a hundred years."

"That's my point. Something a hundred years old couldn't have been made to hold up all the skyscrapers."

"Well, hopefully it will hold up for one more day, just until we get to the riverbank." He nodded towards a loud screeching underground train that was packed with passengers. "This next train is ours, so jump on."

"Look!" I said, pointing at the words on the platform. "It says 'mind the gap'! I never really understood what that meant!" I carefully stepped over the gap between the platform and the train and squeezed onto the quiet car of passengers, most of whom were either reading their phones or the *Daily Mail.*

The train took off, and I practiced my English accent along with the lovely invisible voice that announced the stations as we approached. At the next stop, a slew of passengers exited, and Sam and I sat down on faded blue fabric seats.

"How'd you do it?" I asked him, waving my oyster card at him.

"You did great, Marion. Kind of loud, but it was a good diversion." I rolled my eyes while he continued. "One of the ladies turned to look back at you, and I simply slid her card out of her hand while sliding my card into her hand. She was too distracted to notice. I got the German man's card when I shook his hand to thank him."

"Easy peasy," I said.

"Hopefully, if Blythe is tracking us, she'll go to Buckingham Palace or wherever those tourists are going, and we'll be in an entirely different part of the city. One good thing about London is that there are millions of people to hide among, but there are also more CCTV cameras here than probably anywhere else in the world. If she has access to the cameras, it might be easier for her to find us."

He looked at me. "From now on, we don't want to cause loud diversions. We want to blend in with our surroundings as much as possible. If everyone is taking a selfie with their camera, then we take a selfie, and so forth. Get It?"

"Got it," I said. "We're veery lucky."

"And we need to be veery careful," he answered.

I followed Sam as we changed trains and got on and off at different stops. He said we were taking a circuitous route, but he didn't want to waste too much time underground. We finally exited at St Paul's Cathedral, and my emotions rose as we went up the escalator and up a flight of the stairs. I was in the center of London!

We came above ground, but instead of a cathedral all I could see were tall office buildings and I was disappointed. This wasn't what I expected the city to look like.

"Where's St Paul's?" I asked Sam, but he kept his head lowered and purposefully walked ahead. I lowered my head, too, and hurried to keep up. We made a few turns around modern office buildings and sleek cafes, sharing the pavement with business suits and laptop bags, and then suddenly the sky opened up and the white dome of St Paul's Cathedral towered above us. I was sufficiently impressed with the over-three-hundred-year-old place of worship. I had first seen it as a little girl in *Mary Poppins* and could still sing "Feed the Birds."

We arrived at the grand front steps which led to a massive front door graced with columns. As we looked up, I noticed the Queen Victoria statue in the courtyard in front of the steps. She was wearing a sign that said, "Do not feed the birds." So much for sentimentality.

We circled around the Cathedral which took a while since it was massively sprawled. I could imagine how impressive this church would have been for hundreds of years before the modern skyscrapers were here. "Too bad all these new buildings are here ruining the cityscape," I said in what I hoped was a low voice.

Sam looked up and around. "I like to think they symbolize London's rebuilding after the German Blitz," he said, "and their spirit of not giving up or giving in. As it happens, London is my favorite city in the world, because they preserve the past but also celebrate the present."

"Well, that's a romantic way of putting it," I said. I was happy to be sentimental again.

"Marion, look straight ahead." I could tell he was excited for me. With the Cathedral directly behind us, we faced the famous Millennium Bridge spanning the River Thames. It had opened in the year 2000 but had to be closed immediately for repairs. So many people crossed the bridge the first day, it started to wobble.

The bridge was also familiar since I'd watched all the *Harry Potter* films with my boys. The bridge was in a dramatic scene when the dark wizards wreaked havoc and sinister mayhem on the innocent city. At that thought, I frowned to myself. Blythe and her cronies were the dark witches in my world, and, unfortunately, this was real life and not a film.

Sam took my hand, and we walked across the windy bridge at the same pace as the other tourists. We'd tag along with a group and if they stopped to pose for pictures, we'd attach ourselves to the next family or group. Halfway across, I looked to either side and couldn't help gasping in delight as I took in the other bridges that crossed the mighty Thames. For once, I agreed with my husband—the past preserved along with present was my favorite, too.

A busker dressed as a huge stuffed smiling panda bear came up to us and waved. Sam tugged me onwards. The couple beside us stopped and took a picture of their little girl hugging the panda, and we attached ourselves to another couple who were walking by.

"Look up," Sam said. "Do you see the tall building ahead of us that's made of glass?"

I pulled my gaze away from the river and looked ahead. "Yes, I saw it on the plane. It's the Shard, isn't it?"

"Yes. It looks like broken glass on top and thus the name. The British are quite original like that with respect to naming buildings." We hurried along another few steps. "We need to get to the thirty-first floor. There's a restaurant on that level, the Aqua, but there is supposed to be special doors in the men's and women's toilets that go to the office. I've never actually been there."

Without stopping, he glanced around. "We can guarantee that

cameras and weapons will be everywhere. They will know we are on our way up. But we are the good guys, and I work for this company. The only caveat is that I'm not sure what they'll want to do with you."

I yanked my hand out of his. "What do you mean want to do with me? Like torture me? Brainwash me?" Things had been going so well and now this.

"No, they will want to *protect* you, but I assume they will not want you to go to their top-secret office that I've never even been to. I assume once we're at the Shard someone will make their presence known and take you to a safe place. When we get to the Shard, we'll tell the reception desk that we have a reservation for English at Table 77. That is the code for getting access upstairs. Normal people go to eat there but that's my company's special table."

"OK, that sounds easy enough," I said even though nothing had been easy thus far and this didn't sound easy either.

"Yes, it should be," Sam agreed, "but I want us to have our own safe place to meet just in case. At the V&A there is a jewelry display. We'll meet there after."

"After? After what? The V and A? What's that?"

Sam took my hand again and squeezed it tightly. "No talking right now," he whispered. "We're so close, I don't know what cameras may be around." Something was about to happen. I was starting to sense these moments.

We had reached the end of the bridge. An ugly brick building with a smokestack was in front of us, and I could see Shakespeare's Globe Theatre to my left. My excitement had left me—I was ready to be done. The sky was still overcast and dull, and clouds hovered low in the sky. It started to sprinkle, and we kept walking, merging with other small groups, and winding behind buildings and restaurants toward the towering Shard.

I'd read it is called the "Eye of Sauron" in a London guide book, and I could feel the eyes of Sam's mysterious company looking down on us. I whispered a prayer under my breath. Surely, he didn't work for a bad company. They would know he was a good guy, and they'd just take him in for questioning, relieve us of Elizabeth, and save the world. Some nice spy lady would take me to get a cream tea, and then Sam would meet me there, and we'd fly home. The rest of the spy guys would arrest Blythe, and that would be the end.

Out of nowhere, two bodies flanked us. The woman on my right took my arm, and I could feel something pressing on my neck. "Keep walking," she said, in a familiar voice. "Don't look around or talk, and everything will be okay."

Then I heard Blythe's voice. *Where were all the cameras and police when we needed them?* She pulled the backpack off Sam's arm. "I'll take that, thank you very much."

"And I'll take *you*," said the woman beside me.

"Our friends at the Shard have been waiting for you," said Blythe to Sam. "They are very interested in hearing directly from you about why you turned rogue. I'll make sure they hear the truth from you."

She motioned toward me. "My colleague here will take your lovely wife on a little boat trip. Just in case there are any problems with getting you to talk, Marion will have one of my special phones so she can hear what's going on. She can also use the phone if there is anything she wants to share." I could tell from her voice she was smirking.

"And, just so you know, we've tracked Grandma and Andrew boy. My American colleague is on her way now to pick them up. The gig is up. I assume what we are looking for is in this backpack, but if not, there are three lovely family members who, I'm sure, would appreciate your talking. If you refuse, the bullets will start flying. *Ça va?*"

Sam turned to me, kissed me on the cheek, and murmured, "You've got everything you need with you. See you soon."

He dropped my hand, and Blythe led him away, one arm clasping his and one arm cupping his neck. She made them look more like a couple rather than a kidnapping.

My witch pushed another red mobile in my back pocket, and said in her Polish accent, "Keep that there. You'll want it to talk to Sam and make sure he's telling us the truth."

By now, I was annoyed. On the first day of our trip when Sam was taken from me, I was terrified. This time I was angry.

Sam and Blythe disappeared around a corner and the blonde witch nudged me back towards the river. She walked us to a ticket booth and bought two tickets for a Thames River cruise. It was something I had wanted to do when I planned the trip, but not in quite this way and not with her.

"Where are we going?" I asked, trying to sound assertive.

She poked me again with the gun. "Be quiet. Go down that way."

Blondie and I followed tourists of all nationalities down a ramp where she gave a young man in a sailor costume two tickets, and he told us to have a nice ride. "Mind the gap," I said as we stepped over the threshold and onto the boat.

12

Diamonds and Daggers

The boat was two levels high. The main level had a glassed enclosure for protected viewing of the regal and stellar sites; an open-air upper deck was lined with benches. Blondie escorted me inside the glassed-in area, shoved me into a seat, and sat next to me. She kept the hand with the gun pressed to my side.

This wasn't America where probably half the citizens have carry permits and are always armed. This was in the United Kingdom. Sam told me the Brits have a completely different mentality towards guns and knives than we do. People here were more worried about white vans running over pedestrians than guns.

I thought for a moment. There had been the knife fight at Shakespeare's house, but Blythe, Blondie and Gypsy Girl all had guns. *Where did one even purchase a gun here?* I looked around, sure that the guests on the boat would never dream there was an armed woman poking a gun into my side. *If I tried to escape, and Blondie did shoot me, surely someone on the boat would notice and not let me bleed to death. The nurse in me knew I would need something to tape up an entry wound. It would really hurt, though. What if I lost consciousness?*

Blondie couldn't make me talk, because as Sam had wisely made certain, I didn't know anything. I didn't even know where Bear and Mom were. At the thought of my family, I knew I didn't want to risk getting shot. I needed to use my brain.

The boat's speaker announced what we were seeing. "On the starboard side—that's right for you non-nauticals—is the *HMS Belfast*. She is the last example of a gunner that fought in World War II, and she's come to rest here. You can go on board and tour her from stern to bow."

I smiled. William would love the Belfast, I thought. He liked learning about World War II in history classes, and we'd watched several movies and documentaries together.

I felt a thud in my stomach, remembering that I couldn't think of Wills in the present tense. I had done that for months after the crash, seeing or hearing something I knew he would like or would think was funny and start to text him. Or I'd walk to his room to tell him something.

Denial, pain, sadness, anger, followed by a downgrade to a dull ache. Then it would start again. I realized that during the trip, running around like a secret agent with Sam, I'd had the least amount of pain I'd had in a year.

The worst day had definitely been when Sam told me he thought Blythe had caused the accident, but it had refocused my guilt into rage at her. I wasn't sure if it was just from pure physical and mental exhaustion, or maybe it had been because Sam was beside me every night, but since he'd told me, I hadn't had a single bout with insomnia.

Asians, elderly white people, and a family with a ginger-haired baby took pictures with their phones and pointed out sites to one another, and I let myself imagine what should have been—my whole family sitting here snapping pictures all together.

I felt anger rise up again. This was *all* Blythe's fault. I forced myself to stop feeling sorry for myself and to think.

Focus, I told myself. Sam is in peril. Bear and Mom are, too. Blythe has Sam's backpack, so that means she has what she was looking for. Mentally, I stopped. *If she had what she wanted, then why did she need Sam?* Would she just release him and then call Blondie and tell her to let me go?

Since that was the simplest resolution, I knew by now it would not be that easy. If Blythe was going to keep Elizabeth and go back to join the bad guys, then she would probably think she had to kill Sam to keep him quiet. That meant they would have to keep me quiet, too. I turned slightly to Blondie. "Blythe has what she wants. It's in the backpack. So why are you kidnapping us?"

She ground the gun painfully into my side. "Shut up."

Why did Sam say I had everything I needed with me? Both of the oyster cards were in the backpack, so I couldn't use one to meet him at whatever the "V" and "A" turned out to be.

I heard the familiar ring of a land line, but it wasn't the mobile in my back pocket. Blondie pulled out a black phone. "Yes?"

She listened and turned to me. "Blythe wants to speak to you."

I felt stubborn and wanted to say that I didn't want to speak to her, but Sam's life was in danger. I held out my hand and took the phone.

"What?" I said, no longer afraid. Instead, I was filled with infuriating rage. This woman was ruining the life of everyone I loved and, according to Sam, she wanted to join the bad side and ruin other strangers' lives for personal gain. She made me sick, and I wanted to scream at her. I prayed for help and spoke in a calm, slow voice.

"What do you want now, Blythe? You have what you want, so just let Sam and me go. You'll disappear, and we'll go back to America. It's as simple as that."

"Not quite as simple as that, unfortunately," she replied. "Your Sammy doesn't have my item of interest. It's not on his person and it is not in the backpack. It was a little painful, of course, for him to be searched, or maybe he liked it. His emotions are a bit confused right now."

"Let me speak to him!"

"That won't be necessary right now. He's having a little nap. Aren't you, Sammy?"

Her voice changed from falsely nice to low and firm. "Listen to me carefully, Maid Marion. You obviously know where this object is since you've been with Sam all this time. You have one boat ride to either hand it over to my colleague or tell her where it is. Once we've confirmed and acquired it, you and your little family will be fine. If you don't comply, first your mommy, then your sonny, and then your hubby will bite it, one after another, and it will be all your fault." She paused and I fumed.

"Let me clarify," she continued. "I want this in my hands by the time you reach the dock, and I wouldn't take the entire cruise if I were you. I might have to make your happy fam hurt a bit to keep you motivated, and you don't want that, do you now?"

I thrust the phone back to Blondie, who took it, said, "Yes, will do," listened for another minute, and hung up.

"We are now approaching the Tower of London and Tower Bridge," said the boat's announcer. "Hundreds of years of history are right before you. If you are disembarking here, please wait until the boat comes to a complete stop before moving. Look around you for any items you may have put down—brollies, bags, mobiles, etc."

My ears were ringing, and my stomach was cramping with fear. I could barely comprehend the enormous stone towers and blue bridge gracefully and grandly straddling the river. I turned to Blondie and spoke frantically. "I don't have it. I don't even know what it is. Sam never told me for my own protection. I don't know anything. Please believe me!" Tears now streamed down my cheek.

Blondie showed no compassion or expression at all. "It takes half an hour for this boat to get to Westminster where we disembark. If you don't tell me by then, bad things will happen to your family."

"Please give me twenty-four hours," I exclaimed. Not that extra time would help me.

"I'm going to search you, and if I don't find anything, you have half an hour," said my captor dispassionately.

I needed to think, to plan, to do something. Nurses are trained to take care of emergency situations and not start crying. That wouldn't help anybody. *Get it together, Marion.* I mentally gave myself a shake, a splash of cold water, and a smack to calm down my hysterics.

Sam said I had everything I needed. Well, I had a phone. Could I use it to my advantage? He said to meet him at the V and A. I needed to find out what that was and get there.

"You can search me in the loo. I told you I don't have anything, and I need to use the loo anyway. I see a sign for one right there," and I pointed to the back of the boat at a sign.

Blondie paused a moment, then acquiesced. "No funny business or you will regret it."

"No funny business," I said. Blondie got up first and pointed me ahead of her. She stayed close behind me and held my arm as if I were disabled and needed help walking. I *was* disabled, by the gun poking my arm. *How could all these people not notice my distress?*

Of course, they weren't paying attention. They were all snapping away on their smartphones and pointing at the buildings lining the Thames. I was in the midst of an international potpourri, and yet I felt all alone. I needed a friend.

I thought of Freya. She had been my friend first, then Sam's friend. I still wasn't certain to whom she was loyal, but she had apparently given Sam passports and money.

You have everything you need, Sam had said. Maybe I could use the phone while in the stall. "I need to use my phone," I said, "but I need to use it alone."

Blondie stopped walking. "So, *now* you are ready to talk. That is good. Not so many people will get hurt now. You can talk in front of me, though. I'm not leaving you alone."

"I still have to use the facilities," I said and continued walking. Blondie closed the gap between us and followed me down a narrow staircase to the loo. There was one stall for men and one for women with a shared sink in the common area.

I pushed open the women's stall door and started to go inside. Blondie tried to follow me in, but I shook my head. "You aren't going to want to be in here with me. I'm sick to my stomach." I shrugged nonchalantly.

"First, I will search you," she said, and closed the door behind us.

This answered my question of whether Sam had stolen an actual item or specific information to relay. It was obviously smaller than a breadbox. Maybe it was a tracking device. No, that didn't make sense. But, then again, maybe it *did* make sense, because it seemed like we were always found wherever we went.

I'd been with Sam every step of the way, though, and if Blythe hadn't found what she was looking for on Sam or in his backpack, then he must have hidden it somewhere.

Blondie began patting me down, and just as I hadn't worried when airport security patted me down, I didn't worry about Blondie doing it, because I didn't have anything to hide.

"What's this?" Blondie demanded, patting my front pocket.

I'd forgotten about the syringe I'd nicked from Freya's kitchen. I'd just transferred it from outfit to outfit.

I pulled out the syringe and held it out in my hand. "I have severe allergies. This is my epi-pen. I have to carry it with me and give myself a shot if I come in contact with anything I'm allergic to, or I might pass out or even die."

"That would make my job easier," responded Blondie, waving her hand repugnantly toward the needle. "What else do you have?"

I pulled out the remaining notes I had left over from the airport that I had jammed in my pocket and held them out towards her. Blondie waved them away with almost as much disgust. She was obviously not looking for money.

I put the notes and syringe back in my pocket and held my hand up to my mouth and made myself gag. "I need some privacy now, because I feel sick. But, of course, you're welcome to stay."

This turned out to be more effective than tears. Her face puckered up, and she told me again, "No funny business. I'm standing right outside this door."

I shut and locked the door and sat down. American stalls had a wide space at the bottom, in case a child or patron became stuck and needed to crawl out. I'd noticed in England and France the stalls went all the way to the floor. The privacy was brilliant.

I opened the phone, but the screen was as blank as the one I'd been given in Windsor and looked impossible to use. I called out to Blondie in what I hoped was an authoritative voice, "I need to use the phone privately. Tell me how to how to unlock it."

The door of the stall shook, and Blondie banged on the door. "I told you to talk in front of me. Open this door," she demanded.

I pushed all the buttons on the perimeter of the mobile, and the screen lit up. I needed the passcode.

"I can get you what you want, but I don't want anyone else to get hurt. I need to make one call to get you what you want."

"Four twos," she muttered, and as I tapped the numbers in, the window to the world lit up. She banged on the stall door again. "If you try anything funny, I will not hesitate to use this."

"Please let the wi-fi work. Please let the wi-fi work," I mumbled to myself. An internet browser opened, and I looked up the number for Freya's apothecary shop. "God, please help me," I whispered as I punched in the number.

Just as I heard Freya's voice, the boat sounded its foghorn. I said as low as I possibly could, "Meet me at the V and A jewelry department. I need your help!"

As the horn stopped blowing, I heard her answer. "I'll see you there in three hours," a pause, and then, "You can do this."

I wanted to cry again, but this time with relief. Sam thought I could do this. Blythe and Blondie thought I knew what I was doing. Regardless of their overly high opinions, I had hope. Help was meeting me in three hours.

I knew Blondie would check the phone to see who I'd called, but I couldn't think of another way. "You are done. Come out," she demanded.

I flushed the toilet and slid the lock open. I needed to delay her for another three hours, and I still needed to figure out what and where the V and A was.

Blondie said nothing but grabbed my arm again and pushed me to go ahead of her.

"I need to wash my hands," I said.

As I started towards the sink, the door opened, and two ladies came into the small space with us. One held a London guide book. Before I could calculate the risk I was taking, I smiled brilliantly and asked the woman with the book if I could look something up. What an actress I was becoming, smiling when my world was in shambles!

The woman smiled back. "Absolutely." It was good to remember that there were still nice and normal people in the world.

Blondie scowled at me and nudged my arm with the gun, but I flipped to the back of the book to look in the index. I hoped she would be disinclined from making a bloody mess with two other witnesses in the tiny room.

I flipped to the V section, ran my finger down the page, and read. The V and A was a museum, not a store! Victoria and Albert. I made a mental note of the address and postcode, thanked the tourist and gave the book back to her. Blondie nudged me again, and I walked back up the stairs to the main floor with my captor on my heels.

"Next stop is Blackfriars," the captain's voice said over the loudspeaker. "Disembark here to see Saint Paul's Cathedral or begin your walk with the bard of all bards, William Shakespeare. Visit the The Blackfriar Pub and discover an eclectic selection of real ales and a generous measure of British hospitality. Take all your belongings, including small children. Any children left behind will be made to sweep the galley. Just kidding, all children left behind will be made to walk the plank. As you disembark, you will see a bucket. If you enjoyed your journey or are just glad it's ending, you can place your tips in the bucket. We take all bank notes and all currency. If all you have left are coins, we take the jingly tips, too."

We sat back down in our seats as other passengers got off, got on, and moved around. Blondie leaned near me and said, "The next stop is Westminster. Then your half hour is up. Do you have anything to tell me?"

"I do, but I need to go somewhere first, and then I can give it to you." My words sounded feeble even to me.

"What do you mean you need to go somewhere? Do you know where the item is? Who did you call?" Blondie turned directly to face me, and her eyes narrowed. She was scarier looking than Blythe.

"I can take you there, or of course, I can go by myself and meet you for drinks afterwards," I said with a sarcastic smile.

"You didn't answer my question. Who did you call?" I hesitated and Blondie was sharp. "Just give me the phone."

I reached into my pocket and handed her the phone. I couldn't guess what Blondie would think, because I wasn't sure what to think myself. Was Freya really going to help me, or was she really Blythe's ally? Blondie typed in the passcode, looked at my search history, and the number I called.

"Ha, you called the apothecary shop in Bath. That was a good idea. For me, but not for you." She laughed cruelly and handed me the phone again.

Blondie took out her own mobile and dialed a number. "I let her make a phone call, and she called our friend in Bath for help," she said. "Should I tell her? She wants three hours to get it." She was silent, apparently listening to Blythe's instructions. She nodded and clicked the phone shut.

"I need to know about Sam and my family. Are they all right? If I get you the item what will you do with them?"

"We'll let Sam and your mother and son go. Your friend in Bath is helping us, you know. She told us where to find your mother and son. We don't want any of you. We only want what belongs to Blythe. Sam is the thief, after all, not you. He took something that didn't belong to him and he has to give it back. If he doesn't cooperate or you don't cooperate, then people will start getting hurt."

"*Start?* Start getting hurt? People have already been hurt and died." I wanted to scream, but I whispered it violently in her snake ear slit. I hated this woman. She was not normal or nice. Did Freya really help Blythe get my family? Who was I supposed to trust?

I could trust Sam. He said I had everything I needed, and he said to get to the museum. That is what I had to focus on for the next few hours.

Blondie shrugged again, unmoved by my words. "Do you know where it is?" she repeated.

"Yes, yes, I can take you there. Now will you please let Sam and my family go?"

"Ha! Don't be ridiculous. You give me what belongs to Blythe, and then you can get your family back. We get off at Westminster." She took a mobile out of her pocket and texted on it. I assumed she was updating Blythe that I did have the info, and we were on our way to get it. Hopefully now they would leave Sam alone for a few hours.

"Our next stop is Westminster where you can see the famous Big Ben in the Elizabeth Tower, the Houses of Parliament, and Westminster Cathedral," the captain began, but I stopped listening, because Blondie nudged me to get up and pushed me ahead of her to disembark along with the rest of the boat's occupants.

"Where is it?" Blondie asked bluntly.

My voice was cold. "I need to go to a certain place. We can get it there," I said.

"No funny business. Tell me where it is," Blondie repeated.

"This isn't funny at all. I need to look at a map," I said.

"I can pull up a map on my phone," Blondie said.

"No, I need to look at a real map. I'm doing what you want. Let me find a map."

We walked by the captain, who thanked us for journeying with him, but we ignored his crew and their tip bucket and went up the stone steps to the street level.

I was overwhelmed with the busyness. Seemingly thousands of people were crushed on the pavement, mostly pointing up and taking selfies in front of Big Ben, which was enclosed in scaffolding, or jostling around one another amongst the London souvenir kiosks.

There were double-decker buses covered in advertisements, taxis honking, beggars with dogs, buskers with bagpipes, the London Eye wheeling on the opposite side of the river bank, towering statues and lampposts—not to overlook the picturesque Houses of Parliament and the gothic architecture of Westminster Abbey.

Blondie clutched me closely and as Big Ben rang out two o'clock, she said, "You have thirty minutes."

I confidently bluffed with my best poker face. "It will take longer than that. This is a timed venture. We can't just whisk in and pick it up. We'll do this the way it has to be done." I pointed to a sign off the pavement. "There's a map."

I studied the sign, which showed a map of the area, and worked out the direction to go. It was probably only a 45-minute walk, so I was going to need to walk slowly to give Freya time to get there. I could only hope she was coming to help and not hinder. Finally sure that I had the route in my mind, I stepped back. "OK. I know the way."

Blondie periodically nudged me with the gun just to let me know she was still in charge. I turned onto Whitehall and followed the crowds. Rather than trying to move around groups or families with prams, I slowed my pace and pretended I couldn't get around them.

A young man wearing a Gryffindor scarf and holding a wand high in the air led a group of giggling teenagers in front of me. That would have been a fun tour to take, I thought, and then switched back to the matter at hand. *Had Freya really found my mother and Bear? How could she know where to find them when I didn't know? Would she help Sam?*

I mentally refocused. I couldn't worry about that—I was going to stick to my initial plan and improvise from there. That's what Sam's plans had all seemed to entail during the entire venture: a plan and then a change of plans. The one thing I had to focus on was taking three hours to get to the museum.

Tall white buildings with gorgeous architecture towered on either side of the street. Uniformed guards with assault rifles stood in front of one black-gated building, but people were pausing, taking pictures and some were kneeling to place flowers for a memorial to the people who had died in the latest attack on Westminster. I was hyper-aware that any stranger could have an agenda to hurt the people around us.

I looked down the drive and pointed at a gray and white cat sitting on a doorstep, oblivious to the cameras and guns. "That's Larry, the Prime Minister's cat."

Blondie glared at me and poked me sharply with the gun. I wondered what might happen if I yelled for help to the guards. She must have had the same thought, because she leaned forward and repeated her patented line. "No funny business. Should I call Blythe and ask how mother and son are doing?"

I shook my head no. I wanted her to forget about my family in America. Besides, I thought, she could be bluffing. It was possible—*I* was certainly bluffing.

We passed the crowd at Downing Street and walked by a number of huge white stone memorials to war heroes and other famous English people. Another photo-snapping crowd was grouped in front of a white building called Horse Guards, and I saw two huge glossy black horses with red and gold uniformed soldiers sitting on top of them. Again, I wanted to cry out for help and again Blondie nudged me firmly in the back. "No…"

"Funny business," I said. "Yes, I know."

"Where are you going?" hissed Blondie.

I could see Lord Nelson's column ahead of us, and I could see the map of where I needed to go in my mind. "We need to go there," I said, and pointed to Trafalgar Square.

The square was a swirl of action and energy. Fountains, four huge black stone lions, and white-columned buildings flanked it, and hordes of young people climbed the lions, ran around and shrieked with laughter. The area was energetic, loud, and crowded, and the atmosphere gave me an idea. Sam had told me it's safest in a crowd, because you can blend in and get lost. Maybe I could lose Blondie.

My blonde mind-reader clutched my arm and nudged her little gun at me again. "What are you up to? Where is it?" she asked.

"Sam told me where it is, and I'm taking you there. We need to go that way," I said. I pointed toward the tall Admiralty Arches that led down the Mall to Buckingham Palace.

Just as we were going to cross the street, I spied Big Ben.

"Look kids, Big Ben," I whispered, and tears welled in my eyes. I felt reckless from fear, and I was starving.

"Aren't you hungry?" I asked my captor.

She paused, hardened her face, and said, "Keep going."

The mother in me knew she was hungry, too. "I have to eat every few hours or my blood sugar drops, which makes my allergies worse," I lied. "Or else I will have to stop and give myself a shot."

I completely fabricated a combination of several medical conditions, but from Blondie's reaction to the syringe, I recognized she had a fear of needles and illnesses that many people seemed to have. Most of my job as a nurse was calming anxious children and, sometimes, their even more anxious parents.

We crossed the busy intersection with red double-decker buses and taxis and walked down the Mall towards the Palace. Union Jack flags danced in the breeze above us on grand lamp posts. Green parks flanked the Mall, and just off the pavement I spotted an ice cream lorry. It was a miniature old-fashioned truck, and I paused and nodded towards it.

Blondie hesitated, and then keeping her grip on my arm, she joined the ice cream queue. It was surreal to get an ice cream cone in front of Buckingham Palace amongst happy families and school groups while I had a gun pushed into my arm.

I didn't think I would die if she shot me in the arm. At least, then, all these royal guards and soldiers would notice I was in trouble. I stiffened as I remembered I wasn't the only captive and probably not the only one hungry. My family would probably want an ice cream, too. *Focus, Marion. Get to the V and A.*

Blondie bought two vanilla cones and after she gave mine to me, held my arm and the gun with her right hand while she held her cone in the other.

We walked towards the Palace, licking our treats. *Sugar makes everything better*, I thought. *This might all work out. We could meet Freya, and she will take over, and my family will be released and done with this crazy mess.* And then…*Yeah, really. Because so far, everything has worked out so easily.*

We finally reached the huge Queen Victoria statue and fountain in front of the Buckingham Palace gates. A crush of humanity, even more than at Parliament's Big Ben, surrounded us. Thousands of people holding Union Jack flags stood waiting.

It didn't make sense to me, because I knew from my tourist preparations that the Changing of the Guard ceremonies were held in the morning. Then, I understood.

"There's Queenie! I see her. She's coming!" I heard a woman say.

The gates opened and three black Range Rovers pulled through. I recognized the queen's standard waving on top of the middle vehicle. Blondie and I both stopped walking and turned to watch. She seemed as properly impressed as I was.

I looked through the dark tinted windows and saw, in the middle Rover, Queen Elizabeth wearing a royal blue hat over her white hair and waving a black gloved hand, it seemed, right at me.

The crowd surged forward. Someone bumped hard into us from behind, and Blondie's cornet went flying through the air. As Blondie turned toward the cone, I heard her suck in her breath and felt her grip on my arm loosen. I took the opportunity and ran.

What I did wasn't running, exactly—I ducked and squeezed and maneuvered my way back through the crowds toward the palace. Masses of people were focused towards the Mall and the queen's entourage, so I stayed as low as I could and kept moving. Once again, I fully expected to feel a bullet in my back, but I kept moving anyway.

I pulled the red mobile out of my pocket and dropped it on the park grass. Now they couldn't trace me, but it also meant I couldn't contact Sam. My only chance was to get to Freya.

Blend in, blend in, I muttered to myself. *Don't stand out.*

I knew Blondie was looking for me and would look for someone standing out from the crowd. I dodged my way past the wrought iron and gold gilded Canada Gate and pushed through the crowds to the pavement that followed alongside Green Park. I slowly turned my head to look behind me, but no blonde ponytails stood out, so I kept running. I passed prams, pigeon-feeding elderly ladies, and one teen-aged school group all wearing rucksacks and riotously singing. I felt momentary relief from the distance I was hopefully putting between Blondie and me.

The spectacular Wellington Arch towered before me, which meant I was getting close to Knightsbridge. I slowed to a brisk walk—as the crowds thinned, I felt conspicuous.

As I approached Harrod's, the streets filled up again with more obviously fashionable families—ladies dressed in high heels—rather than trainers—clutching Chanel bags, and their male companions sporting gold watches and shiny black dress shoes. Even the little dogs were dressed for the occasion in spring-colored pastel jerseys. One car was actually covered in Swarovski crystals.

Move at the pace of the tourists, I told myself, but I still crouched low and stayed close to groups. I remembered that Blondie would be looking for my black leather jacket, so I shrugged it off and dropped it in front of a Romanian woman dressed in swathes of black fabric who was sitting on the pavement holding a little paper cup and begging. "Thank you, madam. God bless you," she exclaimed.

"Yes, please God, bless me," I whispered under my breath.

From my memory map, I was fairly certain if I kept walking on Brompton Road, it would take me to the front entrance of the Victoria and Albert Museum, where, apparently, I had everything I needed, and help was on its way.

My mind wandered. Maybe Sam had escaped from Blythe like I had from Blondie and would meet me there. And everything would be all right. I perked up with the thought and the contagious self-confidence of the rich people who surrounded me.

Soon, up ahead, I saw the palatial cream museum ahead of me with its red banners announcing the latest exhibits. I jogged up the stone steps to the front doors and stepped into the foyer. Before I could go further, a security guard swept me up and down with the wand of a weapon detector. He pointed me towards the queue of patrons who didn't have bags to check.

What a sad but necessary fact of life to assume everyone was dangerous rather than truly coming to the museum for a day of culture and arts! It occurred to me, though, that the security probably meant that Freya or Blondie or whomever might be following me wouldn't be able to bring a gun inside.

I walked inside and went to the help desk. "Please, can you tell me the time and where I can find the jewelry display?"

A white-haired lady who could have been the queen's body double answered me in her proper British accent that it was "half three" and showed me on a museum map where I was and where to go. I was a little earlier than the three hours Freya said she needed, but I could scout out the displays ahead of time and look for a hiding place if I needed one.

I walked through shiny marbled halls past white marble statues and richly appointed tapestries, among hushed voices of patrons admiring the art. Then I walked upstairs under the watchful gaze of the magnificently-painted portraits to the first floor where the jewelry was. I couldn't help gasping with amazement. There were two floors of glass displays of jewelry ranging from two thousand years ago until the present day, and no other people were there gazing at the displays except me.

A spiral glass staircase connected the two floors. I half expected Cinderella or perhaps an English princess to walk down in her glass slippers, but I knew either a friend or foe was more likely.

I'd discovered that there was nowhere to hide, so I climbed the glass stairs, hoping to have a better view from above. It was then that I realized I had backed myself into a corner. There was no way to exit or escape except going back down.

For a moment, I felt ashamed. Sam wouldn't have placed himself in a situation like this. I hesitated, still trying to decide where to wait for Freya, and pretended I was looking at a display case of dazzling diamond tiaras. One of them caught my eye—it had the same brown gemstones as the earrings Sam had given me! The warm gleaming stones were displayed in brooches, rings, and earrings in addition to the crown.

Before Sam had given them to me, I'd never even seen this sort of stone before. Apparently fancy ladies through the ages had been wearing them. I reached up to touch my tangible link with Sam, still securely attached by the screws in my earlobes. I couldn't believe I had almost lost them in Paris.

I put both hands up to tighten the screws and froze. Out of the corner of my eye, I saw someone come into the jewelry room below me. It was Freya. I would finally know the answer to my question. *Was she an ally or enemy?*

I could tell she hadn't seen me, so I started to walk down the glass stairs, but I froze again and crept backwards up the stairs as Blondie appeared from another side of the hall. The two women looked at each other, glanced quickly around the room, then up the stairs to me.

"Marion!" called Freya. "Come here. I'll help you!"

Blondie, who was standing behind her, smiled. She pulled out the red mobile I left on the park grass and waved it gleefully at me. "The phone recorded your conversation to meet at the V and A. You were easy to find," she said.

That decided it. I couldn't trust anyone except Sam, but I knew what to do. Raising my hands into the air, I screamed as loud as I could and ran down the stairs toward the two women. From the last step, I dove at Freya and pushed her backwards into Blondie.

We all ended up in a pile of the floor. Yells and punches ensued, but I remained focused on my goal to get away. While Freya and

Blondie continued to tussle, I pulled away and started towards the exit door.

"Marion, wait!" yelled Freya.

I glanced back just in time to see Blondie pull a knife from her ankle boot and thrust it toward Freya. My friend grabbed her side and slumped over. I ran toward the door exiting the jewelry room and made as loud a commotion as I could. "Help, help! Fight! Fight!"

In the confusion, the red mobile had slid across the floor. I snatched it up and ran down the corridor. Guards raced in the other direction. "Fight, fight!" I yelled again, pointing behind me. "Somebody stop them!"

I would surely be on the museum's video cameras, and I needed to get out as quickly as possible. I paused beside a white marble statue of a young man holding grapes, opened the red phone, and typed in 2222. I pressed the first number on the call history, and Blythe answered.

"Well hello, Marion. Are you ready to talk, darling? Sam sure hopes so."

"Yes, I am," I answered. "Meet me on Millennium Bridge at noon tomorrow," I said, and snapped the phone shut. I dropped it by the statue's long marble toes and walked out of the museum.

13

The Eternal Boy

As soon as I got outside, I looked around to get my bearings and saw treetops behind the museum. I didn't have as many cool spy skills as Sam, but I could find my way around from years of practice as a Girl Scout and as a den mother for Wills and Bear.

Sam wanted the boys to be in Scouts, but then he was never in town to do the activities with them. The summer before my dad was diagnosed with cancer, he'd chaperoned a weekend camping trip with the boys. Even though he wasted away over the next year, the boys, mercifully, only seemed to remember the weekend and all the other camping trips they had gone on together.

It made me feel better to think that Bear had camping and wilderness survival training in case he and Mom needed to hide somewhere in the woods.

Then, I remembered that Blythe said they had already been caught. Realizing there was nothing I could do about it, I pushed the distracting thoughts of my family away.

From the map, I suspected the trees were part of nearby Kensington Gardens. I kept my head down and speed-walked towards them. I made sure to blend in with the happy families, romantic couples, and tourists with maps strolling through the grassy areas and borders abloom with flowers. I let my thoughts wander for a moment—if I hadn't been on the run from a mad woman who wanted to destroy my family, the park would have been a lovely spot for a British summertime picnic.

I had told Blythe to meet me at noon on Millennium Bridge off the top of my head, so I obviously didn't have a firm plan. But I felt safer in the park and, as I walked, ideas began coming together in my mind. I stopped at a sign with a large map of the gardens.

First, I needed to get some make up. Maybe the Duchess of Cambridge or Sussex was in residence at Kensington Palace, and one could lend me an eyeliner pencil. Likely not, but you *do* read about Harry going for a run in the park or Duchess Catherine taking the new prince out for a stroll in his pram.

What would I do? Go over, and say, "Excuse me, your majesty, but I am an American who unknowingly married a spy who is working for a company in London, and he's been kidnapped, and I am running from his crazy former colleague. Could you please help me?"

It was a fun fantasy, but I shut it off and followed the path along the Long Water with the aim of walking through the garden and out on the other side. A commotion near the water revealed a group of enormous swans and little ducks surrounding children with bread crumbs. One child, obviously frightened by the eager- ness of the swans, threw his baguette in my direction. I picked it up and tucked in under my blouse for dinner later. Sometimes you have a snack with—or near—the queen, and sometimes you, well, eat dis- carded bread. I had certainly learned to be resourceful.

I passed a picturesque Peter Pan statue in a gated garden and a fountain with two bears hugging, and finally arrived at a grand wrought iron exit gate. I kept my head down, because I had no idea if cameras were in the park and on the street, and I was certain the museum guards were going to be looking for me in connection with Freya's death and Blondie's arrest.

My stomach lurched at the memory of my old college roommate falling over with the knife in her side. What about her darling children and husband? Did her husband know she was a spy, or had he been kept in the dark like me?

Again, I refocused myself on the immediate plan. I walked along a grand street running parallel to the park, under mature leafy-green trees and flanked by graceful white Edwardian buildings. Outside a flower-laden pub called The Swan, I stopped briefly to read its historical plaque.

The pub had been a coaching inn dating back to 1721, just a young pub compared to the one we had seen in Canterbury. Further down the plaque, I read that the pub was reputed to have been the final drinking place for victims on their way to be hanged. The phrases "one for the road" and "on the wagon" had been coined there.

Today, though, the front garden was filled with wooden tables of happy drinking customers eating meat pies and chips, but I had the happy thought of Blythe on the end of a rope.

I passed a stone church tucked in amongst white hotels flocked with colorful window boxes and boxwoods, and finally saw what I needed—a drugstore.

I bought dark foundation, kohl eyeliner, eyebrow color, a red lipstick, and false eyelashes, which left me with just a ten-pound note. The next shop was filled with London souvenirs and a handwritten sign promoting scarves that were five pounds each. I picked out three black ones and went to the dark-skinned man at the till. I held out my tenner and the last of the coins I had.

"This is all the money I have left. May I please get these three scarves?" He shrugged and took the money, and I left the shop wondering why we don't haggle in Ohio.

The end of this seemingly endless day was finally arriving. It was getting darker and colder outside and was time for me to find a safe place to sleep. I would need to get some other things before my rendezvous with Blythe, but I could finish "shopping" in the morning.

Keeping my head down, I went back into the park. I put one scarf around my hair, one around my neck and shoulders, and the third around my torso and the top of my legs like I was wrapping up with a towel after a bath.

I knelt beside the bear fountain, cupped my hands under the flowing water, and drank the refreshing water. There was a special basin for dogs, which were certainly treated like royalty around here. I saw that even their waste had its own royal-looking red and black painted iron receptacle.

Pausing, I watched tourists with their maps and phone cameras, locals either jogging or walking their dogs, and students kicking a football, and wondered what happened in the park at night. A sign posted on the entrance gate said the park closed at dark.

I thought of a bedtime story I once read to the boys about Peter Pan in Kensington Gardens. The story said that any children left behind in the park at night were taken care of by fairies. I certainly needed a fairy. Surely there weren't enough guards to sweep the four hundred acres of the park every night. This was one of the few areas I hadn't seen any beggars or homeless people. Maybe the night-time fairies indeed took good care of them all.

I walked through hundreds-of-years-old trees lush with green foliage, lawns crisscrossed with footpaths lined with flower gardens, and stopped by the Peter Pan statue, which shows him playing his flute above a tree stump that hid rabbits and fairies and noted that it was surrounded by low trees and bushes. I entered the gated area surrounding the statue, pushed aside some of the bushes, and ducked under some tree branches that hung low to the ground. Once I was under the tree, the space opened up, and I could stand. Some rubbish was scattered around, so I knew my hiding spot wasn't unknown, but hoped no one would come if they saw I was there. Kind of like "first come, first hide."

Settling on the ground with my back against the tree trunk, I pinched off the end of the baguette and tossed it aside—in case there were swan or little boy germs on it—and slowly savored the rest, one bite at a time. It seemed ages since I'd had the ice cream, and the bread tasted truly delicious. I hoped that the rest of my family was being cared for by the fairies that take care of kidnapped people.

I could hear people all around me—conversations in different languages, British and American accents, crying children, and barking dogs, but no one disturbed my foliage room. As it got darker and quieter, I wrapped my scarves tightly around me, prayed for Sam, Bear, and Mom, and with the comforting thought of night fairies protecting me, I fell asleep.

A few times throughout the night, I woke up—from strange noises, to move an uncomfortable branch or pebble under me, or to adjust my scarves to cover exposed parts of my body. But overall I slept until I woke to the faint streaks of a pale sun and the sounds of birds and squirrels up early to socialize and eat breakfast.

I could hear grass-cutting machines and blowers—the gardeners working early to make the park pretty—and I suspected someone would soon come to collect the rubbish under my tree.

I rewrapped the scarf around my head, upper body, and torso, and made my way through the bushes past Peter. "Thank you," I whispered to the eternal boy, and thought of Wills, who would always be *my* eternal boy.

I hurried to the public toilet at the gardens entrance, which was beginning to feel like my front door. I didn't have coins to pay to enter, but since no one was around, I crawled under the turnstile. I added this to the record of wrongs I attributed to Blythe. I would pay extra on my next visit.

After splashing my face and trying to scrub my teeth clean, I applied the dark foundation and red lipstick, thickly lined my eyes with the kohl liner, and darkened my eyebrows. Once I stuck on the false eyelashes, even I didn't recognize myself.

I tied the scarves around my head and body in my best imitation of a Muslim woman and prayed for forgiveness for unintentional disrespect. I closed my eyes, waited a moment, and opened them again. *Who was this woman in the mirror?* She certainly didn't look like an American soccer mom.

Step one of my two-step plan before meeting with Blythe was complete. From my experiences over the last week, I knew step two would most likely not work out as I planned, but it was all I had.

I exited my "front door" back onto the tree-lined street and crossed over to Lancaster Gate tube station. Tourists with suitcases, traveling Londoners, and workers with laptop bags crowded around the oyster card machines.

Distract and switch, I told myself. Pulling my scarf low over my eyes and purposefully going to the front of the queue, I cut in front of a blonde woman who was about to put her credit card in the machine to buy an oyster card. With my black shawl covering my hand, I pretended to tap my card on the reader.

"Excuse me, it's my turn," the nasally American said and pushed my hand away with her card.

"Sorry," I mumbled in my best British and moved behind her.

The American completed her transaction. Her oyster card came out of the slot in the kiosk, and she started to put her credit card back in her wallet.

"Sorry, you dropped this," I said and waved my hand wildly with the end of one of my black scarves. She turned to me, and I held my hand towards hers—the one with the oyster card—and pulled it out of her hand.

"Hey, stop! That's mine," she said loudly. The station worker walked towards us to see what was going on between us. I hurriedly gave her back the card.

"Here, here, you dropped this," I said and then fell over. On the way down, I grabbed at her to catch myself and I saw her credit card fly out of her hand. I swiftly picked it up and tucked it away. I was clearly not as smooth as Sam, but my second effort paid off.

She glared at me, looked down at her oyster card, shrugged and muttered about idiots and rude people as she got up and walked away.

Before she'd realized I had taken her credit card, I hurried back outside the station and flagged down a black cab. "Do you take credit cards?" I asked as I climbed in the back.

"Yes, Madam," the cabbie answered, and I instructed him to take me to Piccadilly. I needed crowds, confusion, and costumes for step two, and Piccadilly Circus contains all of these.

As I emerged from the taxi, I was energized by the noise and activity level of all the people and vehicles. Piccadilly is the British version of New York's Times Square. It was not my favorite part of England, but it served its purpose. No one glanced at me or pushed past me. I felt invisible as I glided through the crowds behind the protection of my veils.

I stopped to speak to a shop security officer. "Sorry, please, do you know where I can find a fancy-dress shop?"

He pointed me down the street with explicit lefts and rights. Focusing on everything he said, as if he were a doctor giving life-saving instructions for one of my patients, I followed the directions and ended up at a shop in the theatre district. I walked past tart and pirate costumes, past the Elizabeth and Darcy finery, to a side aisle filled with head and body-covering costumes—bananas, gorillas holding bananas, bananas holding gorillas. I turned and my eyes lighted on the perfect costume—a larger-than-life-sized Mr. Fox.

Fantastic! It was a male character, would completely disguise me, and suited my needs for anonymity perfectly. I carried it to the front till and filled out pages of paperwork swearing upon my mother's grave to return the costume. Otherwise, I would be having "one for the road" at The Swan before I hung from the gallows of Marble Arch.

"Going to a fancy-dress party?" asked the tattooed man behind the counter. He was dressed as Jack Sparrow.

I nodded. "It's for a charity event. You know, Cure for Juvenile Diabetes? We have a fun run and then a party for the children."

"Nice one, that is," he responded, even though I'd made it up. "You need to be careful not to wear this too long in the heat. Take the head off to get a breather now and again."

I lowered my eyes demurely like the proper Muslim woman I pretended to be, and Pirate Man continued. "Look, here's a brilliant feature," and he pulled up a little flap near the paw. "It's storage for your mobile or wallet or whatever you need. Most don't have something like this."

"They are going to be completely knocked out and dazzled and intimidated by me," I responded with a smile.

"Fantastic," Pirate Man said and gave me the bill.

I solemnly swiped the Tube lady's card, promised myself I would repay her somehow, and walked out of the shop with Mr. Fox.

The Anchor and Crown Pub was down the street, but before I went inside to change clothes in the ladies' room, I remembered that a proper Muslim woman would be very unlikely to go into a pub. Beside it, there was a Costa coffee shop, and I went inside the innocuous café and into the ladies room there. I quickly changed from my Arabic persona to Mr. Fox and stuffed the scarves inside the sleeves of the costume in case I needed them later.

I tried to read a coffee patron's mobile to see the time, but my vision was mostly blocked by the inside of the head. The costume was intended for males, so the eyeholes were above my eyes. Another customer noticed me leaning over and said, "Hiya, Mr. Fox, what can I do for you?"

"Can you tell me the time, mate?" I said in as deep a voice as I could manage.

"Trade you the time for a selfie," the man said, so I leaned in for a photo while he snapped and told me it was half eleven.

"Thanks, mate," I said and sauntered to the door. It was hard for me to grasp the doorknob with my paws, so another customer hopped up to help me.

I was beginning to think the Mr. Fox costume wasn't the best idea after all, but I was stuck with him now and needed to get on the Tube and to Millennium Bridge. At the station, two older gentlemen had to pull me through the train car doors after the conductor blew his whistle at me for blocking the exit.

What slowed me down most were small children and teens

coming up to hug me. My "anonymous" costume was causing way more attention than I had intended, and several children and parents asked to take pictures with me. From all the smiling, hugging, high-fiving, and fist-bumping reactions, I suspected I had chosen the costume of a beloved movie hero.

Through it all, my stomach felt queasy from worry and fear about Blythe. Dads and mums pressed coins into my paw which I thought I could use to reimburse Tube Lady, but instead, I clumsily dropped the coins into the open guitar case of a busker who was strumming and singing as I exited the Tube along with hundreds of other politely-queuing passengers.

The busker promptly thanked me politely and profusely as all the beggars in this well-mannered country did. I hoped the circle of life concept worked out favorably with me thieving and redistributing wealth like Robin Hood.

I went carefully up the stairs at the tube station at St Paul's, but had trouble holding Tube Lady's card and tapping the card reader with my paw until a little girl happily helped me. I emerged above ground once again and retraced Sam's and my steps to Millennium Bridge, all the while amazed that it had only been the day before that we'd walked across it together.

By this time, my worry and fear were almost overwhelming. *Would Blythe have a gun and shoot me? Would she knife me to death like Blondie had done to Freya? Would she be on the bridge at all?* Maybe Sam had broken down and told her where Elizabeth was, and all her pony-tailed girls were about to surround me and do terrible things to me.

I waddled onto the gleaming metallic bridge and gripped my supplies in my paws. I prayed I would be dexterous enough to complete my plan and cursed myself for choosing such a complicated costume. I started to cross the bridge and immediately encountered the same unwelcome attention I'd attracted in Piccadilly. Families with children swarmed to hug me, take pictures, and press pounds into my already full paws.

Then, out of the corner of my eye, I saw a woman in black with a blonde ponytail striding confidently across the bridge towards me. It was Blythe. She paused halfway across the bridge and pulled a red phone from her pocket. Maybe, I thought, she was checking the time or coordinating diabolical schemes with her cronies.

One good thing was that Sam wasn't with her. Thinking about him gave me courage, and an idea popped into my head. I walked straight towards her and put my massive furry arm around her shoulders.

She tried to step away from me. "What are you doing? I don't want a picture. Let go of me!" she said. I turned my grinning face toward her and squeezed her shoulder again. "I said let go of me," she said again, and rudely tried to shake my paw from her shoulder. A little boy yelled to his mother and ran toward me. "Mum, look! Can I give him a hug?"

It was now or never. I'd given hundreds if not thousands of shots to children over the years and quite perfected the art of hiding the needle. With Freya's syringe in my hand, I pushed it through the opening in my paw and jabbed the needle into Blythe's chest. She gasped and turned towards me and, as she crumpled to the ground, I saw a hint of recognition in her eyes.

I lumbered across the bridge, ignoring the other children calling out to me, and made my way through the old streets and markets towards the Shard.

14

A Reservation

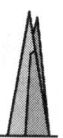

Much to the crying dismay of two ginger-haired twin girls, I pulled Mr. Fox's head off outside the Globe Theatre. I stepped out of the rest of the brown fur suit by the Clink, wound the black scarves back around my head and body, and became a shrouded woman once again.

I kept the gleaming tower of glass in view and purposefully moved forward. The sky had been overcast all day, and I felt a few drops of rain. It would be just my luck if my make-up started running.

Although my plan had worked, I couldn't believe it. All I could think to do was complete the task Sam had set out to do twenty-four hours before—turn myself in.

"Are you eating at the restaurant, madam?" asked the security guard holding a clipboard at the front door of the Shard.

"Yes, I have a reservation for English at Table 77," I heard myself say with unusual confidence.

"The lifts are straight ahead. The thirty-first floor."

"Thank you," I said and entered the gleaming modern lobby.

The lift shot me to the top, and I could see all of London before and around me. The sights would have once delighted me, but without my family, they all seemed stupid and meaningless. And somewhere down there amongst millions of people, my Sam was hidden.

I exited the lift and told the hostess I was meeting my party but needed the loo first. She directed me around the corner, and I entered a marble sanctuary. The room was surrounded by mirrors, and ensconced in warmly lit marble. Somewhere in there was an office door and I would have to find it.

I went in the first stall, sat down, and looked around. There was a control panel on the wall where one could press a button to warm the seat, produce a gentle cleansing stream of water, or give more loo paper. One by one, I went into each stall, waiting impatiently as patrons took their time.

The seventh stall was identical to all the others. I pushed the seat warmer, then the gentle rinsing button, and then an emergency call button. That was different.

This was indeed an emergency—I had a possibly-kidnapped son and mother, definitely-kidnapped husband, a possibly-dead enemy on a bridge, a stolen credit card, and guilt for not having returned the Mr. Fox costume, which would result in a large charge on the stolen credit card. The pleasure I had brought to strangers as Mr. Fox and the absolute joy of the thought of Blythe lying on the bridge could not make up for everything bad that happened.

I hesitated, pushed the emergency button, and a mirrored panel at the back of the tiny room slid open. I hesitated again, pushed open the door, and went through the looking glass.

In front of me was what seemed like a typical office reception. A gray-haired woman tapped away at a computer at the front desk and business-suited men and women hurriedly walked through, talking to one another or texting on their phones. I went to the front desk and said, "I'm Sam Martin's wife, and I need to talk to someone in charge."

The receptionist jumped up. "Yes, Mrs. Martin. Marion, isn't it? Please follow me." She led me down a corridor to an office, knocked on the door and pushed it open. "Sam Martin's wife to see you."

I stepped in to see my college roommate sitting behind a large mahogany desk. She stood and rushed toward me with both arms open. "Marion!" she exclaimed. "You made it!"

"No, Freya," I mumbled sarcastically and stepped aside. "It looks like *you* made it." *Was this another trick?*

Freya carefully pulled up her blouse and showed me a large white bandage. "I *did* get stabbed, but I was wearing a bullet-proof vest. The knife pierced through but not as far as it would have. Kind of ironic—a bullet wouldn't have hurt me."

"Yes. Ironic."

I shook my head. "I give up. I just give up. I know what you want. And I have it, and I can give it to you. Just kill us all, I guess."

She laughed gently. "No one is going to kill anyone. You, Sam, and I are all working together. I'll explain. But first, where's Sam?"

Now I was even more confused. Freya hadn't asked for the prize first, although I had told her I had it.

"He's…I don't know. Blythe took him, and Blondie—you know the lady with the knife—took me. I…I killed Blythe, I think, on Millennium Bridge, but I don't know what she did with Sam before that."

Freya frowned. "All right, first things first. I'll have our friends with the London police pick up Blythe and question…what did you call her? Blondie?"

"And Bear and Mom! They're in trouble, too!"

Freya picked up her phone and started issuing orders.

I started to interrupt her, but she stopped me and covered the mouthpiece. "Let's get your family taken care of first, and then we can talk."

Two men in suits came into the room, and the three conferred and started typing on their computers and talking on their phones. After a few minutes, Freya turned to me. "The good news is that your mum and Bear are just fine. We have them in custody."

Suddenly I felt weak and turned around looking for a place to sit. Freya rushed to support me under my arms and signaled an assistant to get me a chair. When I sat down, the tears started.

"They're okay? You have them in custody?" I couldn't make sense of what was happening. "You've arrested them?"

Before Freya could answer, the receptionist who'd let me in knocked on the door again. "Marion Martin's husband to see you, madam." The door swung open and Sam rushed into the room.

"Marion!" he yelled, and then nodded in Freya's direction. He crushed me in a hug and then held me away from him and looked at my outfit. A hint of a smile crept onto his face.

"What are you wearing?"

My strength suddenly renewed, I twirled around while he unwrapped my scarves and then hugged me to him again.

Freya laughed. "She did really well, Sam. Our cameras didn't pick her up. We thought it was one of our field agents coming in. And...she says she put Blythe down."

"I know," he said, rocking me gently back and forth. "It's how I was able to get away. Blythe left me with one of her guards when she went to meet Marion. My guard got a call that something had happened to Blythe and then took off running. Nobody was left—I just walked out of the building where she was keeping me."

"We all have a lot of explaining to do," said Freya, "so let's sit down and talk. What do you need? A bite to eat? Water, tea, whiskey?"

"Yes," we said in unison, and then burst into laughter.

I looked at Sam and gestured at Freya, who was perched on the front of her desk. "They have Bear and Mom. They're fine, I think."

Freya nodded. "Yes, both Andrew and Mrs. Worthy are in our safe hands. I pretended we were tracking them down as a way of establishing trust with Blythe, but I was really ensuring their safety."

"How did you know where to find them?" I asked, still hurt she knew more about the whereabouts of my family than I did.

"We lucked out on that," she said, chuckling. "Andrew ran a red light. Leave it to teenage drivers."

I hadn't heard anything funny, so I didn't laugh.

Freya continued. "Male drivers of that age have the worst driving statistics. The UK delays the driving age to seventeen, but the stats are bad until age twenty-five." She saw my expression, slid off her desk and pulled a chair near us.

"The police pulled him over to give him a ticket, and when they ran his license and registration, it alerted our computers. We easily found them from there, pulled him over again, and after a rather lengthy conversation—I had dialed in to reassure them— the two were convinced that my field agents were there to help them and not harm them. Right now, they're sequestered in a hotel in Kentucky."

Sam nodded and chose not to ask any more questions, so I followed his lead. The receptionist came in with a tray of sandwiches, water, cups of tea, and three glasses—each with an ice cube—into which she poured generous portions of whiskey.

One of Freya's male assistants entered the office and nodded at each of us in turn. "Madam, madam, sir. I'm sorry to interrupt, but we've just had a call from America. Andrew Martin and Mrs. Worthy are on their way to the airport."

Now I was even more confused. "The airport?"

"Yes," answered Freya. "After I saw how upset you were, I thought you'd want to see them as soon as possible." She turned back to her assistant. "Thank you, Sean. Any news on our friend Blythe's colleagues in America?"

He shook his head. "It seems they've all done a runner like Mr. Martin's guard. As soon as the word got out that Blythe was dead, all her colleagues scattered."

"All right, we will follow up on each one of them. Has our police friend gotten access to Blythe's body?"

"I'm working on that," he said, and then left the room.

Sam looked at me. "Mar, I'm curious. How did you manage to kill Blythe?"

I shrugged. "Well, it's a long story, but the end of it is that I dressed in a Fantastic Mr. Fox suit and met her on Millennium Bridge. I injected her with poison I stole from *her* house." I pointed at Freya.

Sam and Freya looked at each other, then back at me. "Where did you get the suit?" asked Sam.

I started to cry. "I'm just as bad as Blythe. I'm a thief and a murderer. I stole a woman's credit card to rent the suit at a fancy-dress store, and now I won't be able to return the suit because I took it off on the way here."

"Wait," said Freya. "You injected Blythe with poison you got from my house?"

I nodded. At least she hadn't said stolen.

"I thought that was Blythe," she said.

I shook my head. "No, it was me. I knocked over all that stuff in your kitchen so you would *think* it was Blythe."

She burst into laughter. "Well, your plan worked." She glanced at Sam. "I told you she would be good," she said.

Then she looked back at me. "And if you used what you took from my house, then you *didn't* kill Blythe." She picked up her phone and punched in a few numbers and one of her assistants appeared at the door.

"Blythe isn't dead. She'll wake up within twenty-four hours," she said. "Marion injected her with a Juliet, so she can't be left alone—in a morgue or anywhere—or she'll escape when she wakes up. We have to move fast."

"I'm on it," said her assistant, and he dashed out of the room.

I wiped my eyes and stared at Freya. "I didn't kill her?"

"No, you didn't kill her. That's actually good—once she's awake again, we can hold her legally accountable for all her crimes and she'll go to prison. And, Marion, don't worry. Our company will make restitution for the credit card you borrowed."

"And the fox costume," I said.

Freya nodded and laughed. "*And* the fox costume."

She walked to the door of the office. "Now you two eat and drink and let me and my colleagues do their jobs from here." She looked at Sam. "We'll explain everything shortly, but first, I'll give you two a few minutes alone."

When she closed the door, Sam pulled me into his lap and held a half-sandwich up to my mouth. I took a bite and, giggling, held a cup of tea up to his mouth. He sipped it, and said, "Ah, there's nothing like a refreshing afternoon tea on our British holiday."

The tension and stress began leaving my heart and body, and I lay back in his arms. We ate and drank and laughed and ate and drank again. After a few minutes, Freya's assistant opened the door and handed Sam a tablet. "Look who's on Skype."

Bear and Mom were smiling and waving to us from the screen. "We're on our way there," Bear said with excitement in his voice. "Gramma said I'd get back home in time for classes."

My mother laughed. "Yes, I did. But we hate to intrude on your romantic vacation."

"We don't mind," I said. "We'll worry about your classes and everything else later." We waved good-bye and blew kisses to each other. It would be so good for us to all be together.

Freya returned and sat down behind her desk again. "I have an update. We have Blythe under arrest at the prison hospital. We caught her colleague at the V&A earlier and our surveillance cameras are tracking down her other companions."

"Sounds good," said Sam.

We freshened up in the office loo. It wasn't as luxurious as the Shard restaurant's, but there were toothbrushes, combs, and I was able to get the kohl eyeliner off with lotion and a wash cloth. I felt almost normal when we all met together again in Freya's office.

"Let's talk now," she said. "All the loose ends are being tied up, so what are your questions?"

Before I could even get started, Sam said, "I think I understand what happened. Blythe went rogue, which is obvious now, but she came to you and said *I* had gone rogue. You had to test us both to see who was lying."

"Yes, exactly. If you said something, Blythe said the exact opposite. You were both partners for so many years and knew each other so well, you each had the inside knowledge to make the other sound like the enemy we were searching for."

My old friend looked at me and smiled. "What's interesting to me is how well Marion, Andrew, and Mrs. Worthy handled all this. You were all quite brilliant."

Sam waved his hand around the room. "It looks like you've done well too. You've obviously been promoted. Congratulations."

Freya looked slyly at him.

"Thank you, Sam, but I actually got this promotion seven years ago. It has been part of my cover to continue as a field agent and keep in contact with all my colleagues and with 'Isengard Headquarters.'"

Sam and I laughed at the reference to the Shard and *The Lord of the Rings*.

"What happened to the gypsy girl?" I asked.

Freya's face grew solemn. "In this war, Marion, sometimes foot soldiers do fall. When we tracked you to Paris, I sent an agent to connect with Sam. Sadly, you know what happened to her, but thankfully because of her and Sam, we were able to help the Paris authorities thwart an attempted terrorist attack.

"And…I was there, too. The reason I needed you to give me three hours to meet you was because I was in *Paris*—not in Bath."

Freya returned to her seat behind the desk. "And that brings me to the point of this entire mission. A certain tiny object that's worth a lot of money. Blythe needed funds to start anonymously and richly anew. Do we all concur that it's time to hand it over to our collaborative government agencies for inspection and safe keeping?"

Sam looked at me. "I do if Marion does," he said.

"Yes, I do," I said.

I reached up and unscrewed my beloved brown topaz earrings. "I believe these are what you're looking for."

Sam grinned. "I *knew* you knew," he said.

"And I *knew* you knew I knew," I said. "You hinted about the jewelry collection. And when you said I had everything I needed with me, I remembered how twice during this escapade, you had me take out my earrings."

I handed the earrings to Sam who passed them to Freya. "I'll get you some new ones—better ones. I promise," he said.

"You'd better." I laid my head on his shoulder.

Freya carefully placed the earrings in a brass box and locked it in a safe behind her. Then, she cleared her throat. "Now, this is the difficult part."

Sam and I both sat up.

"A major component of our job is secrecy," she said. "Secrecy for our own protection and that of our families, our clients, and our colleagues. Your identity is blown now, Sam, as is mine to you." She paused. "However, seventeen years of service is invaluable. Your wisdom, expertise, and loyalty can't be replaced. What if I made you an offer?"

"We're listening," responded Sam.

I couldn't help being pleasantly surprised that he'd said "we."

Freya grinned. "That's exactly my idea. The two of you together, maybe your entire family. They managed to not only trust and obey orders, but they were able to think on their feet, hide in plain sight, and come to the right side. And, if you're in agreement, when Andrew and Mrs. Worthy get here, we'll send you four on a family holiday—a Mediterranean cruise, perhaps. Then we can meet again, discuss our options, and…future assignments."

Sam and I looked at one another.

"What are you thinking, Mar?"

I paused and took a deep breath. "I'm thinking I need to go shopping for cruise wear."

~ The End ~

Made in the USA
Middletown, DE
25 September 2019